# DIRTY WORK

## Dirty Deeds: Book One
## By TA Moore

ROGUE FIREBIRD
PRESS

Published by Rogue Firebird Press

This is a work of fiction. Names, characters, places, and incidents
either are the product of author imagination or are used
fictitiously, and any resemblance to actual persons, living or
dead, business establishments, events, or locales is entirely
coincidental.

Print
Printed in the United States of America
First Edition
March 2022

*Dedication*

To the Five, all of us for now and always. I love you all and appreciate everything you've done to support and encourage me. And to my mum, who puts up with my brain being away in other worlds a lot!

And, of course, to C.S Poe. Who knows why!


*Acknowledgements*

Thank you to Penny Rogers and Brian Holliday for keeping me on the editorial straight and narrow, even in the gross bits! I know I make you go 'ew' but at least I'm not writing in annoying fonts anymore!

# CHAPTER ONE

**IT WAS A DIVE** bar restroom in bumfuck, Kentucky. Grade had set his expectations low before he pushed the door open. Turned out that "low" was still too high.

The dead man lay sprawled on his back on the tiled floor in a puddle of his own blood. One side of his head was gone. Well, not gone. Most of it seemed to have been splattered over the doors of the stalls, hair and bits of bone shellacked over the greasy mess of graffiti left behind by past customers. The man was barefoot and hadn't taken the care of his feet necessary to make that choice.

On the other side of the corpse, a man in well-worn jeans and a sleeveless tank top pissed into the bloodstained urinal.

"Christ," Grade said, the exclamation dragged out of him involuntarily.

The man glanced around. He took the cigarette out of his mouth with his free hand and gestured at the corpse.

"First time?"

"No," Grade said. He shrugged his kit bag off his shoulder and let it thump down onto the tiles. "I just didn't expect to find anyone else in here."

The man shrugged.

"I needed a piss."

Tattoos covered his shoulders and down his arm, mostly professional-looking instead of stick-and-poke jailhouse scribbles.

That meant he wasn't here because he couldn't afford to drink anywhere else. So either he was slumming or…

"Are you Ezra?" Grade asked.

The last drops of urine hit the porcelain, and the man gave his cock a shake before he tucked it away. He took one last drag on his cigarette, flicked it into the urinal, and then tugged his jeans up over lean hips so he could zip up.

"What business is that of yours?" he asked, his voice still lazily good-humored in that slow, easy way that around here meant the opposite.

The back of Grade's neck felt sweaty and uncomfortable. "I was told to ask for Ezra."

"And now you have."

They both waited. After a second, the man snorted. He stepped over the corpse and gave his hands a brisk wash in the sink. Habit made Grade silently sing along, and the end result wasn't exactly pandemic proper but close enough.

"Ezra's in the office," the man said. He shook water off his hands and then wiped them on his jeans. "I'll tell him you're looking for him."

He took a long step over the puddle of blood and walked toward Grade. Three steps, and then he paused. They stared at each other expectantly. Grade was mildly surprised to realize he was taller and…

…in the way.

He was in front of the door.

Grade stumbled to the side, nearly tripped over his kit, and had to grab the wall to keep from losing his balance. He snatched his hand back quickly and tried to ignore the itch that started at the base of his fingers and worked its way down to the heel of his hand.

"You know, you should still wear a mask," Grade said. "Especially in a confined space."

The man raked curly light brown hair back from his face and tucked it behind his ears. His smirk was crooked but creased the corners of his dark brown eyes. "Like Covid could survive in this shithole," he said. "It's syphilis you have to worry about."

He pushed the door open and sauntered out.

Grade waited until he was gone, the door swung shut behind him, and then rubbed his hand roughly down the leg of his chinos. The fabric wasn't nearly abrasive enough to make him feel certain that layer of skin was all gone.

It was fine, he told himself grimly. That wasn't even his best hand. He could get along without it.

He scratched his palm absently as he assessed the space and started to put together his plan of attack. The door opened behind him and bumped into his back.

"Fuck sake," Grade snapped as he turned and yanked the door open. He glared at the rangy, harsh-featured man on the other side. "It's out of order."

The man looked Grade up and down, snorted, and tried to push past him. "Go fuck yourself."

Grade put his shoulder to the door to keep it shut. "There's a free beer in it for you," he said.

That worked. The guy grinned, suddenly loose and friendly, and took a step back, his hands up to prove he wasn't going to push it.

"Hey," he said. "Whatever you say, man. I can piss outside."

He turned around, which involved more footwork than was necessary, and headed for the side door.

A woman perched on the stool at the bar, dark brown hair loose over her shoulders, waited for him to stagger outside, then shook her head.

"Hate to break it to you," she said. There was something familiar about her, which wasn't a surprise. Sweeny was a small town. Grade just couldn't quite put his finger on how he knew her. "But he had a good idea of what was in there. It wasn't exactly low-key. Guy goes into a bathroom and doesn't come out for over an hour, you gotta hope he's dead."

The barman got a bottle of Common from under the bar and flicked the cap off. "In that bathroom?" he said. "*I'd* hope I was dead."

The woman laughed as she stole the beer for a swig. Despite the roll of banter, her hand was shaking as she picked up the bottle. Her knee bounced in time with the tremor.

Grade ducked back into the restroom to drag the miniature yellow "Closed for Cleaning" A-board out of his kit bag. He shouldered the door back open and set it down outside with a clack.

"You want to work with someone taking a crap on your workstation?" he asked.

The woman laughed. "Just be grateful that Hadley didn't have chili on the menu tonight," she said as she braced her elbow on the bar. She winked at the barman. "God knows, Hadley is. Otherwise people might blame him for the dead man in there."

The barman—Hadley—looked unamused as he peeled a toothpick and put it between his teeth.

"It's not my chili," he said. "I get it from a jar like God intended."

"Just don't let anyone in," Grade said. "I need to go talk to Ezra."

He nudged the A-board into place with his foot and started across the bar. He paused as something occurred to him and turned back around.

"Oh, and whoever took his shoes?" he said. "I need them back."

The woman and Hadley traded looks quickly. Then the woman craned around to look down at Grade's feet. "I don't think they'd fit you."

That got a snort of amusement from Hadley. Grade made an exasperated noise. He wasn't in the mood.

"They're evidence," he said. "Get them back."

The woman rolled her eyes at him and went back to her beer. The barman just shrugged. Grade left them to it as he stalked off to find Ezra.

It was a job, he reminded himself. Money in the pot. He'd done worse.

He just missed LA, where the restrooms were nicer and the criminals were professional. Unfortunately, it was hard to have a shoot-out over Zoom. So here Grade was. Back home, again.

Fucking pandemic.

§

Adam Ezra had his sleeve rolled up, bloody cuff tucked up to his elbow, and his hand braced on the desk. His arm was laid open in a long, ragged gash from his wrist all the way up to his elbow. Blood splattered over his paperwork in messy smears and blotches. The man from the restroom stood hip shot in the corner of the room as he poured two glasses of better whiskey than they served outside into tumblers.

"Just find the bastard," Ezra snapped into the mobile he held in his other hand. "What was he thinking? This is going to cause a goddamn war—"

He stopped as he caught sight of Grade. "I'll call you back. Just get on with it," Ezra told whoever was on the other end of the call and hung up on them with a jab of his thumb against the touchscreen. He focused on Grade. "Who the fuck are you, and what do you want?"

Restroom man took a swig of whiskey straight from the bottle, gave the mouth a cursory wipe, and twisted the lid back onto it.

"Oh yeah," he said as he turned around. "I meant to tell you he'd gotten here. This is the cleaner."

He handed Ezra one of the tumblers and hooked his foot around the leg of a nearby chair to pull it over. Ezra sniffed the liquor and grimaced before he fixed his attention on Grade.

"You old enough to be *in* a bar?" he asked.

"What, the Slap started to card people?" Grade averted his eyes from the gory mess that was Ezra's arm. "And I'm twenty-six. For the record."

"Great." Ezra tossed back the full glass of whiskey in one gulp. He hissed softly and wiped the back of his good hand over his mouth. "So why are you in here instead of getting rid of my problem?"

"I get paid upfront," Grade said. "And what do you want me to do with the body?"

Ezra made an aggrieved sound. "What, do you think I'm picking out hymns? Get rid of him. And for fuck's sake, Clay, get on with it."

Clay pulled a battered camo-print bag out from under the table. He unzipped it and pulled out a heavy-duty surgical stapler. He took the second glass of whiskey and poured half of it over Ezra's arm. The sting of alcohol on raw flesh was enough to make Ezra swear and try to pull away. Rather than let him, Clay grabbed Ezra's wrist, fingers folded over the heavy gold watch, and casually ran a row of staples along the cut to seal it together.

The sight of it made Grade's stomach turn, and he shifted his focus to the other side of Ezra's face so he could only see the bloody arm in his blurry peripheral vision.

"I think he means, do you want the body to disappear," Clay said, between the solid *ker-thunk* of the stapler, "or turn up in a field somewhere?"

Ezra closed his eyes and sucked in a breath as the metal pinched down on raw flesh. His hand tightened around his phone until his knuckles turned white and sharp-looking under his skin. Sweat broke on his face and ran down onto his collar.

"Ah, fuck, you're a goddamn butcher," he accused Clay through clenched teeth.

"You want a good job, go to a hospital," Clay said. "You want an interesting scar, I'm your man. There. Done. Jesus, you'd think I cut it off."

He finished the job with one last staple, dunked the stapler into the whiskey, and grabbed a roll of gauze to wrap around Ezra's arm. It was safe to look, now the whole mess was covered, and Grade was briefly distracted by how nice Clay's hands were. Under the scars, ink, and tan—which were not negatives either— they were long-fingered and elegant, even when bloody from impromptu surgery.

The thought of *that* was enough to make Grade feel vaguely off-balance again. He swallowed and cleared his throat.

"I take cash or money transfer," he said. "No checks."

Ezra pulled his arm away from Clay and stuck the tape down over his hairy forearm himself. He glanced at Clay and gave an impatient jerk of his chin toward the bottle of whiskey.

"You get paid when the job's done," he said. "Not before. What if you're incompetent? Prove yourself and I'll give you a nice bonus. Free night at the Chicken Choke, all the lap dances you want."

"My sister works there," Grade said. That made Clay snort—then shrug when they both looked at him—as he handed what was left of the bottle to Ezra. "So no, thanks. I prefer money anyhow, and I find people are a *lot* less willing to pay up once the mess is gone."

Ezra took a quick, hard pull on the whiskey and then smacked the bottle down on the desk. He wiped the back of his mouth on his hand.

"Or if you don't do what I want, I'll shoot you too," Ezra said.

Grade stuck his hands in his pockets. "Then you'll have two corpses."

"He's got you there," Clay said with a chuckle.

"Get the fuck out. Do something useful and help find TJ before he screws us all over," Ezra said flatly. He waited until Clay did as he was told, the door clicked shut behind him, and then pulled a worn billfold out of his back pocket. It took him a minute to flick it open and fumble through the bills with one arm not cooperating. Finally, he pulled out a handful of notes, folded them between his fingers, and held them out to Grade. "Make sure you do a good job. I wanna be able to eat off the floor in there when you're done."

Grade took the money and thumbed through it quickly.

## DIRTY WORK

"That's up to you," he said. "But I just do bodies, not catering."

# DIRTY WORK

# CHAPTER TWO

**CLAY SCRUBBED BLOOD** off his hands in the kitchen sink. The bar of soap was thin and piss yellow. It smelled of coal tar, and that took him back. He let his brain idle in neutral as he picked the blood out from under his nails.

It was one of the things the military had taught him, right after the fact that no matter what the recruiter had promised, a high school dropout from rural Kentucky wasn't going to be on the fast track to fuck all. Luckily, the second lesson had made the first more bearable: soldiers didn't need to think. Not on a daily basis. In fact, a lot of the time, it was better if you didn't.

That's what basic training was for: getting rank-and-file recruits to the point they could get on with the job without their brains having to check in more than once a day. Everything was rote. Everything was practice. Break down that rifle thirty-two times—fingers raw as the oiled black parts were spread over the table—and then put it back together again for the next recruit in line.

The military wanted soldiers to *do* and officers to *think*.

And if the officers weren't holding up their end of the deal, well, best not to think about that.

Clay dried his hands on an old T-shirt and turned to look at Arlo Hall, pinned down in his chair by Harry's heavy tattooed hands clamped down on weedy shoulders. Under Clay's gaze, Arlo shifted uncomfortably on the hard plastic seat and gulped, the bob of his Adam's apple jerky and exaggerated in his wasted throat. His lip was split, and one eye was halfway to swollen shut.

It wasn't that Clay had any compunction about hurting people. He didn't get off on it like some, but it would be specious to pretend he had any moral qualms at this point in his life,. He found it was just best to run on instinct and not second-guess himself.

"I told you I didn't know where he was," Arlo blurted out as he cringed down as far as Harry would let him in the chair. He licked the sweat off his upper lip. "Me and TJ ain't joined at the hip, y'know. I just slip him some cash to run errands. That's all. He's his own man."

Clay pressed his damp thumb between his eyebrows and sighed.

"He's your son," he said.

The blank look he got was all he deserved, he supposed. Arlo had the emotional range of a catfish. It wasn't even the pills or the booze, although Clay figured they hadn't helped. Everyone who'd grown up with the asshole, and in someplace as small as Sweeny, that was nearly everyone, said he'd been like this since he was a kid.

"OK, let's try that again," Clay said. "We're not done here, Arlo. I'm just done punching you."

Most people would have enough going for them to realize that was a threat. Not Arlo. He wasn't even smart enough to hide the smug look as he thought he'd gotten away with something.

Idiot.

"Jesus Christ, Arlo," Clay said, shaking his head as he pushed himself upright. "You're a piece of work."

He punched Arlo in the face. His knuckles mashed Arlo's lumpy nose, which folded in on itself with a wet crunch and a spurt of blood. The blow knocked Arlo back in the chair, the front legs briefly up off the ground before Harry tightened his grip and brought them back down with a crack.

"What the 'uck," Arlo slurred through his fingers as he reached up to cradle his nose. His voice thick and snotty as blood dripped down his needle-scarred arm. "You said you were done punchin' me! Wha' happened to tha'?"

"You made a liar out of me, Arlo," Clay said. He wiped his hand on the leg of his jeans and nodded to Harry. The big man hauled Arlo and the chair over to the turned-up-to-the-max stove. It had been a while since it had been cleaned—if ever—and yellow globs of grease had melted off the tempered glass door and splattered over the floor. "Tell me something, you stupid fuck. Did you think we were going to roast some veg for your Sunday dinner?"

For the first time, worry crossed Arlo's face as he looked back over his shoulder. He tried to squirm away from Harry, his whole body contorted into tight, awkward shapes.

Leaving Harry to keep Arlo from lizarding away out of the chair, Clay circled them both and pulled the door of the oven open. It was red-hot and the heat blasted out to scorch his knees. Arlo had left half a tray of ribs in there, and they'd cremated, the meat turned to charcoal and sauce baked into a crust. It smelled like it had already gone bad before the oven had been flicked on.

"What are you doing?" Arlo demanded. He dug his nails into Harry's hands as he tried to squirm out of his T-shirt. "I told you. I don't know any-fucking-thing!"

"Yeah, but I don't believe you," Clay said. "So if I were you, I'd think of some-fucking-thing to tell me before I see how much of you I can cram in here."

He slapped the top of the stove. It was greasy and hot enough from the oven to sting.

Arlo swore, a desperate, slurred run of filth, and kicked desperately at Clay with grubby sneakers. One wild kick caught Clay in the thigh hard enough to hurt, and the next slammed the oven door shut.

"Ha!" Arlo yelled. "Fuck you. There! What you gonna do now?"

Clay stared at him for a moment. Some days the people he had to deal with made him regret throwing his lot in with Ezra. Not that he'd had another option.

Still, for fuck's sake.

He reached down and pulled the door open again. "That," he said.

Arlo tried to kick it closed again. This time Clay grabbed his ankle before he could connect and hung on.

"Where would TJ go if he was in trouble?" Clay asked slowly, in case that was the problem Arlo was having.

Arlo licked chapped lips and sniffed. "Fuck you," he said, his voice strung tight with nervy defiance. "You ain't gonna do shit."

When Clay didn't immediately "do shit," Arlo's lips twitched into a smug-bastard grin. He wasn't a man that had many wins in life, so Clay gave him that one… for a second. Then he yanked on Arlo's leg hard enough to drag him half off the chair and shoved his foot into the oven.

The tray of ribs cracked against the back of the oven as Arlo's foot jammed in awkwardly between the two shelves. Grubby rubber melted against the hot metal, and Arlo squealed as the pleather trainer blistered and peeled.

"All right!" he screamed. "I'll tell you, alright? I'll tell you!"

Clay nodded. "Go on."

"Damn." Arlo writhed around in the chair, hands clamped down and white-knuckled on the arms. His face had gone a sickly color. "The fucking lake. The thingy one, like a dam, up by the mines. Cave Lock Dam. My da used to take him fishing up there. Stupid wee bastard was too dumb to wonder why they never caught any fish. TJ goes there sometimes, hides out in the shack."

His words had slurred together at the end, spat out as quickly as Arlo could get them off his tongue. Sweat dripped off his face as his foot scorched.

Clay supposed that was *something*. Not much, but enough to at least make it look like Clay had put the effort in. He caught Harry's eye and gave him the nod to let Arlo go. The minute he did, Arlo slid onto the ground, with a crack as his tailbone hit the tiles, and he yanked his foot out of the oven

He tried to pull his charred shoe off with both hands but snatched them away as the hot rubber blistered his fingertips. Arlo whimpered at the pain and tried to scrape the overheated trainer off against the floor

"Hey," Clay said. He snapped his fingers to get Arlo to look up at him. "Wash your fucking feet, Arlo. It smells like shit in here."

He stepped over Arlo's legs and headed for the back door. Harry waited long enough to give Arlo a kick in the ribs.

"And next time, keep your nails to yourself," Harry told him.

§

"Look at it," Harry grumbled as he stuck his arm out. Bloody scores ran across the back of his hand. "What am I going to tell Lanie about this?"

They were parked in the car just down the road from Arlo's house, tucked into a dirt road pull-out under the trees. Crickets chirped in the undergrowth, and a particularly huge one had dropped with a *thwap* onto the windshield a minute ago. Clay watched it idly out of the corner of his eye as he hung up on the man he'd sent up the mountain to look for TJ.

He didn't like bugs. He hadn't liked them before he went on tour in Afghanistan, liked them a whole lot less afterward.

"Cat?" Clay suggested as he put his phone away and got a smoke out. He flicked the flint on his lighter. It sparked twice before it caught. He lit the cigarette and sat back, exhaling blue-gray smoke into the cab. "Raccoon?"

The acrid taste of smoke on the back of his tongue, the heat of it in his chest, grounded him in the static of his thoughts. It always took him a while to get his brain back on the tracks after turning it back on. It puked up a dozen different ideas at once, like a toddler who'd had too much ice cream.

What the fuck was TJ thinking, killing the goddamn Catfish Mafia's man in the fucking bathroom? Do it outside.

At least the cleaner was pretty, with his lemon eyes and green-smoke smell…

…what the hell? No.

Shouldn't have called him in, whatever color his eyes are. It'd be better to come clean and grovel, but fucking Ezra has fucking pride.

Green eyes. He had green eyes, and he smelled of lemon bleach. That makes more sense.

Was it too late to pick up some BBQ ribs from the Chili's on the interstate?

He ignored the scattershot explosion of thoughts and took another drag on his cigarette. Next to him, Harry pointedly turned the car back on so he could lower the window more.

"If a fucking cricket gets in," Clay said, "I'm going to make you eat it."

Harry put the window up about half an inch. Still plenty of room for a cricket, but that was on his head.

"What am I supposed to do?" Harry asked. "Tell Lanie I tried to catch her a raccoon that was a heavy smoker?"

The corner of Clay's mouth curled up. "Some girls like that sort of thing."

"She's not a girl. She's a woman," Harry said dryly. "And since when do you know what women like?"

Clay flicked ash out the window. He'd thought about tapping it onto the floor, but he liked Harry. The big man was good at his job and could hold an actual conversation… and hopefully, once the thrill of getting back together with his ex wore off, he'd discover a topic other than Lanie again.

"She was a raccoon at that Halloween party Ezra's mom threw," Clay said. He held up his free hand and counted his points off on his fingers. "She works at a wildlife rehab place. Her phone case has a raccoon on it. Unless she's got a tattoo that says 'Secretly I hate raccoons' on her vulva, I don't see how fucking her would enlighten me about what she likes."

Harry grunted and put the window down again. "Don't talk about fucking my wife."

"Ex-wife."

"Fuck you."

"You ain't my type."

Harry snorted. "Please," he said as he licked his thumb and smoothed his eyebrow. "I'm a catch."

Clay laughed around his cigarette and then held up his hand as the phone balanced on the dashboard started to ring. TJ had left it in his jacket, hung over the back of a seat in the main bar when he went for a piss. Then he decided to just murder the bagman for the biggest deal Ezra had ever gotten a sniff of and leg it out the back, with a brief stop to lay Ezra's arm open with a switchblade when he'd tried to grab him.

It made no sense, but fuck it. Half of the people Clay had killed had been complete strangers, so who was he to judge.

The contact that flashed on the screen said "Dad," which was pathetic enough to make Clay feel a bit bad for TJ, even after the mess he'd made of Clay's night. It might be biologically accurate, but expecting Arlo to play any sort of role other than loser was wishful thinking.

He clamped the cigarette between his lips as he picked up the phone and swiped it on. For a second, he blanked on what TJ would say. After a glance at Harry—whose shrug passed the buck back—Clay went with a strangled, whispered, "Yeah?"

"What the hell did you do, boy?" Arlo raged down the phone. "Two of Ezra's boys were just here, that gay one and some big fuck, asking questions and trying to put the screws on me. Everything I've done for you, and you bring this shit to my door? Your mom should have listened to me and taken the damn pills to get rid. You hear me? Whatever you done better have been worth it, because you're going to need to make this up to me. Where are you?"

Clay turned his mouth down at the corners in a disappointed grimace. It *was* confirmation that Arlo didn't know anything, which was useful. Clay had just hoped for more.

"Just outside," Clay said. "And I think we put those screws on pretty good, Arlo. Now throw the phone out the window and learn to mind your own business."

The sound of Arlo's breath rasped down the phone into Clay's ear.

"Go to hell," Arlo snarled after a shocked moment. "What the *fuck* you gonna do about it?"

Clay leaned back and stretched his legs out in front of him into the deep footwell. He leaned over into Harry's side and pressed down on the steering wheel. The blare of the horn made the cricket jump off the car, and Clay swore to god, if it got in through his window, he'd shove it up Harry's ass.

On the other end of the line, he heard the replay of the horn.

"I could come back in," he said.

The line cut out. Clay shook his head and tossed the phone into the pocket on the door next to him. It could rattle around with the spare change and drink lids. Clay had no immediate use for it, but someone with more brains than Arlo might try and call TJ.

"One day, someone is going to call your bluff," Harry said dryly as he pulled out of the lay-by. The car jolted as the tires ran over the deep ruts dried into the ground after the last rain. "Then what you gonna do, Clay?"

That's what he liked about Harry the most. Harry still thought Clay was bluffing.

"Let's hope we don't have to find out," Clay said. He meant it too. Lanie made a good pot roast, and in Clay's experience, when he did have to follow through on a threat, dinner invitations dried right up. Clay flicked his cigarette out the window into the dark. Hopefully, it would hit that fucking cricket. He leaned back in the front seat and closed his eyes.

"Drop me off back at my car. I'll go tell Ezra what's gone down."

# CHAPTER THREE

**GRADE DIDN'T USUALLY** do toilets, but here he was, arm deep in a U-bend. The bleach covered most of the smell, but the fact there seemed to be barnacles under the rim was a bit off-putting. He tried to ignore them as he shifted position to get his shoulder into it.

Almost.

He felt his fingers start to cramp as he twisted his wrist at an odd angle and strained just that little bit closer…

His fingernail caught on the sharp edge, and he—carefully—pulled the tooth up the slick, curved side of the bowl.

"Little bastard," he said as he turned it over in his hand to check if there were any other bits to find.

It had broken off at the root—probably when the bullet had smashed through the corpse's skull—but the rest of it was intact right down to the filling. Grade dropped it into a small jar with the rest of the bits and pieces he'd collected. Then he flushed the toilet and wiped it down for fingerprints before he left the stall.

He closed the warped, graffiti-covered door behind him and pulled a handful of antibacterial wipes from the industrial packet he'd brought with him to scrub down his arms and hands. His knuckles were red and itchy from the chemicals—*or the syphilis,* he thought as he remembered Clay's crack and then tried to pretend he hadn't—but he was almost done.

Just a few last touches.

There was a spare pair of gloves left on top of his kit bag. He dried his hands and then pulled the thin latex on with a tug at the fingertips to get the fit snug. The playlist that filtered through his earbud switched from pop to country rap, with the hard beat of the song enough to give him a boost of energy for the last few minutes. He hummed along absently as he fished the pipes out of the oxygen-bleach bath and reattached them. Plumber's tape sealed them up neater than they'd been before. The bleach then went down the drains, and he left that to fizz while he rolled up the bloody plastic sheets and shoved them into bin bags. The doors he'd taken off to scrub down had to be reattached too, braced with one shoulder as he jiggled the hinges into place.

Once everything was done, he took a second to appreciate the squeaky-clean bathroom. Then he set about making it look like nobody had cleaned in here since 1963.

A spray bottle of piss and shit—Grade aggressively didn't think about that—gave an appropriately disgusting patina to the urinals and toilets. Grade got down on his hands and knees, which ached despite the pads, and rubbed dirty grease into the grout and over the tiles. Once that was finished, he turned back to the stalls. Most of the graffiti had survived being bleached, but a few had faded. Grade pulled a couple of Sharpies out of his pocket and touched them up. He gave in to temptation and added an unprofessional dig at one of his old high school bullies.

It wasn't like he signed it.

Done.

Grade hesitated for a second. Back in LA, he'd have trusted himself on that, but it had been a while since he'd had a full cut-and-scrub like this. He stripped off his jumpsuit—PPE was in short supply still—and balled the stained fabric up to stuff in the bag with the rest of his gear.

No, he'd thought of everything he could. Time to clock off. He checked the time. Not quite dawn. He'd worked fast.

Grade stretched both arms above his head, fingers linked together, until he felt the knot between his shoulders unravel. Then he started to pack everything up. Flammable items— clothes, hair, stained fabric, fingertips—in one bag, non-perishables—rings, teeth—in the other. Grade tied them up and dumped them in the drum he had already loaded onto the dolly. It was heavy enough he had to throw his weight against it to move it, but once it did, it was easy enough.

One foot hooked the door open, and he dragged it out into the bar.

The last stragglers had gone home. Only the barman and the woman, who'd donned a miner's heavy jacket to ward off the chill, were still there.

"Thought you might need a hand," the woman said. She pushed the plate of congealed nachos she'd picked over to the barman and hopped off the stool. A wry smile played over her face as she shrugged. "Buchanan was a big man, and you're… well… not."

There was a trick to not retaining information. It was like unfocusing your eyes, just a slackened muscle that let what people said wash over Grade's brain without leaving an impression. The trick was easier if Grade knew not to pay attention, but he still did his best not to take any note of the name or how memorable it was.

It was best not to know.

"Thanks, but I'm fine. This is what I'm paid for," Grade said. He leaned over and slapped the side of the drum. It made a heavy, stuffed sound. "And our mutual friend is more travel-sized now. I can get him out to the van easy enough."

The woman looked queasy. People did, sometimes. Oddly enough, even the ones who'd made the corpse, as if disposing of someone was somehow worse than killing them. She rubbed the back of her neck and looked away.

"I'll call Ezra and let him know you're finished," the barman said. "Do you need anything?"

Grade braced his sneaker-clad foot against the bar at the back of the dolly to hold it in place. He pointed his chin to the heavy double doors into the bar.

"Could you get those for me?" he asked.

The barman wiped his hands on his apron and came out from behind the bar. He stretched his legs to get to the doors ahead of Grade and pushed them open, stoppers kicked under both to keep them open. Grade wheeled the remains outside and bumped it down the two steps to the parking lot.

"You're Pulaski's boy, right?" the barman asked suddenly. "How's he doing?"

Grade nearly tipped the dolly over as he fumbled the turn in surprise. He leaned forward to grab the top of the drum and pull it back. The weight shifted inside it as it settled back against the uprights of the dolly. It had been a while since anyone had asked him about Tommy Pulaski.

"Still missing," he said.

The barman chuckled and pulled a crumpled packet of cigarettes out of his back pocket. He tapped a slim cylinder out and lit up. The paper flared, and the tobacco glowed dully as it caught.

"Sure," the barman said, cheeks hollow as he took a drag. He exhaled a cloud of gray-white smoke that drifted upward into the predawn light. The sharp mint smell made the bugs veer away from him. "Missing like a fox, eh?"

He winked at Grade as he took another long draw on the cigarette. Then he stubbed it out on the rail and took it back inside with him.

Grade leaned on the duct-tape-reinforced handles of the dolly and shoved it up the ramp. Irritation gave him a burst of energy to make it easier.

There weren't a lot of good things about having a probably dead dad. That people felt sorry for you was about all you got. Except Grade didn't even get that, since everyone assumed he was in on some sort of ten-year-long con. Like his mom scrubbed down toilets and cut old ladies' fingernails just to keep up appearances.

But a good story was better than a miserable truth, Grade guessed.

He strapped the drum into place and jumped out of the back of the van to fold the ramp back up. Once it was out of the way, he slammed the doors and headed around to boost himself up into the driver's seat.

One good thing about being back in Sweeny, he didn't have as far to drive to dispose of the remains. Grade started the engine, and the playlist switched from his ear to the stereo system. He reversed out of the spot and pulled out into the road to the breathless beats of Perfume Genius. It was fifty minutes up the road to the old lake.

With any luck, he'd be home in time to get a couple of hours in bed before his mom got him up to make him breakfast and tell him he'd wasted his potential.

That was the curse of the "gifted child." It didn't matter how much money criminals paid you to destroy evidence for them; if you weren't a doctor, your mom wasn't impressed.

§

A possum paused in the middle of the road. Its eyes gleamed yellow as it was caught in the beam of the van's headlights. It abandoned whatever roadkill it had dined on and scuttled to the side of the road. Grade glanced after it. He'd driven this road a hundred times. More. The muscle memory of that much repetition meant he could probably drive it in his sleep.

Hell, he probably had back in the—

Lights flashed in his eyes, bright enough to blind and so *close*, and then the pickup smashed into the side of the van. Grade felt weightless for a second as he was thrown to the side, only anchored by the seat belt that cut into his shoulder. He came back to earth, thrown into the door as the van spun around on the road. The forest and the road flickered through the windshield like a flipbook with out-of-order pages.

"Shit."

Grade grabbed the wheel and tried to wrestle the van back under control. "Steer into the skid," that's what the driver's ed instructor had always said. Maybe that was only if the road was wet, because it did Grade no good at the moment. His wrists ached as he tried to stop the wheel from being yanked back and forth, but it just spun out of his hands.

The van crashed into the barrier at the side of the road and scraped along it. Sparks flew as metal struck off metal, stripes of factory-issue white paint visible on the corrugated steel. Grade slammed the brakes on. Or tried to. The pedal just smacked down against the floor, but nothing caught.

After one last sickening lurch, the van came to a stop.

Grade grabbed the wheel. He clutched it in sweaty hands for a second and then realized that wasn't going to help. It took a moment longer to convince his fingers of that, but he finally managed to get them to let go. He reached down with one hand to fumble at his seat belt and pushed the driver's door open with the other. It popped free, and he half climbed, maybe mostly fell, out of the cab.

There was blood splattered over the driver's side window. Grade panicked for a second and then realized it was his. He gingerly ran his hand over the side of his face to find the gash as he took a step away from the van. There was a split in his forehead, just over his eyebrow, where he must have bounced it off the window.

The pickup was stopped in the middle of the road, headlights smashed and bumper crumpled from the impact. As Grade squinted at it, the passenger side popped open, and someone scrambled out.

"On your knees!" the man yelled. He clutched a gun in one hand and jabbed it in Grade's direction for emphasis as he loped forward. "On the ground. Get down on the ground."

Grade hesitated for a second as he weighed his options. It didn't take long, but it still made him too slow for the man on the road. He lowered the gun and pulled the trigger twice. The bullets bounced off the ground in front of Grade's feet, splinters of concrete sharp against his ankles.

"Down!" the man snarled. "Now."

Grade slowly did as he was told. "There's nothing worth stealing in there," he said as he lowered himself down onto one knee. "Just some old clothes and bleach."

That's what it said on the side of the van anyhow—Spare Sock Laundry. It had been on it when Grade saw the vehicle at auction, back in LA, and he'd figured that was even more nondescript than an unmarked van.

The man snorted as he crab-walked forward. He had a cap pulled low over his face and a bandana wrapped around his mouth. Grade could see the damp patches where the man's breath had soaked into it.

"Lying bastard," he said, and brought the gun down in a short, vicious punch. The heavy metal and plastic cracked against Grade's skull, and he went down. He had a second to register the growl of the pickup as it raced off and hands on his shoulders as he was rolled over onto his back. Then everything went black.

§

Cheap whiskey burned Grade's sinuses and stung the back of his throat. It tasted like the backyard moonshine one of his mom's boyfriends used to cook up. He spluttered, choked the mouthful down, and pushed the flask away from his lips before he got another shot.

"What the—" he muttered, and then he remembered. "Shit."

Clay took a drink from the silver flask before he capped it and tucked it into his jacket. He offered Grade one of those unexpectedly elegant hands—the knuckles now split and bruised—to pull him onto his feet. Grade stared at it for a second and then took it. The trip from prone on the road to upright made his head spin and his stomach throw sour bile up into the back of his throat. He pulled his hand out of Clay's and stepped to the side, doubled over with his hands braced on his knees as he waited for the sick heat to pass.

"Tell me you just blew your wages tying one on," Clay said.

Grade closed his eyes and let his head hang down. He took a moment and then pushed himself back upright.

"No such luck," he said.

Clay stared at him for a second and then turned around, hands on hips, to scan up and down the road. He saw the same thing that Grade did.

The van was gone, along with the disassembled dead man.

"Well, fuck," Clay drawled, slow and sticky as his accent got clotted up with the night's bad luck. "Just when I thought this night couldn't get any worse."

# DIRTY WORK

# CHAPTER FOUR

**RAGE MADE A** vein throb in Ezra's temple, but he kept his voice down to a low snarl. He had the kids this weekend, apparently. They were asleep. He had been too, from the fact that all he had on was a pair of hastily dragged on sweatpants.

"You. Lost. It?" Ezra asked, each word pushed out through his gritted teeth. He stepped onto the porch and closed the door behind him. "How the hell do you lose a corpse?"

Clay could have answered that. For once, though, he wasn't the one in the firing line. Grade shifted his weight uncomfortably and rubbed the back of his neck. The quiet confidence from his last confrontation with Ezra had been lost. He seemed uneasy, off-balance. Either he didn't get in trouble very often or it was the blow to the head.

Maybe both. It wasn't like Clay had taken him to the hospital. He'd just given Grade a couple of Tylenol and some mouthwash as a chaser.

"Someone caught me on the Blackfish Line," Grade said. "Drove me off the road just before the Peele and Hooker intersection. They had guns—"

"You have a gun," Ezra snapped.

"I don't."

Ezra's eyes bulged. He reached for Grade but pulled back at the last minute and balled his hand into a fist instead. He pushed his knuckles hard against his mouth and made a frustrated sound. Clay could sorta sympathize.

"You don't have a gun?" Clay said.

Grade turned from the waist to look at him. The lump on his forehead looked tender, the edges of it stained purple as the bruise came up. "I don't like guns."

Clay scratched his eyebrow and pulled a dubious face. "It's a gun," he said. "It's like a Grindr hookup. As long as it gets the job done, it doesn't matter if you like them or not."

That earned him a quick, speculative look from Grade. "If I had a gun, they'd have shot me," he said.

Ezra grabbed his face, fingers and thumb pressed into the lightly tanned skin of Grade's jaw.

"That wouldn't be a me problem," he said. "Would it?"

Grade clenched his fist for a second and then stretched his fingers out again. "They'd still have the van, so I don't see how you'd be any better off."

Ezra pushed Grade away from him roughly.

"I'd feel better," he said as he turned to stride restlessly along the porch. The old waxed boards creaked under the heavyset man's bare feet. He rubbed his fingers over his forehead and up into his unruly sandy hair. "You try to get ahead, and every bastard is just there to tear you down. And this moron doesn't have a gun. You know who he is, Clay? This baby-faced asshole?"

He stopped mid-pace and pointed at Grade, just to make it clear who he meant. Grade pulled a sour face but held his tongue for once.

Clay leaned back against the porch, one hip hitched up on the handrail, and his booted foot dangled in midair. He held the flask of whiskey in one hand, metal warm against his fingers, and tapped it against his leg as he shrugged.

"The cleaner?" he said.

"Tommy Pulaski's kid," Ezra said, with a sort of bitter triumph. Then he grimaced and waved his hand irritably as he turned his back. "You don't remember Tommy Pulaski, do you?"

Clay shook his head. "Maybe before my time."

"He was a thief and a con-man," Ezra said, with pointed cruelty in the boiled-down description. "And he ran off with a cool million stashed in his car. So the family has form."

The sharp line of Grade's jaw tightened as the jab hit home. He licked his lips and swallowed hard before he said anything.

"I'm pretty sure Dad's dead," Grade said. "Even if he wasn't, I think meth has a better resale value than a corpse."

Ezra turned and crossed the distance back to Grade in two long strides. He grabbed Grade by the shirt, fingers twisted into cotton, and shoved him into the wall of the house. Grade's sneakers scuffed the wood as Ezra pushed him up onto his tiptoes.

"That's because you," Ezra said, his voice dangerously calm all of a sudden, "don't have a fucking clue who you just cut up."

Clay pushed himself to his feet, tucked his flask into his back pocket, and walked over. He put his hand on Ezra's arm. The muscles were clenched tight, and Clay could feel the heat of the recently stapled-back-together gash in his forearm through the gauze.

"Ezra," he said. "Your kids are snitches. You want Janet on your case about bringing work home on the nights you've got custody?"

He wasn't sure why he bothered. The tall, scrawny cleaner was cute enough—in a frat boy wannabe way—but Ezra was his business partner. They went way back. Far enough that they were still friends, even if they didn't like each other much anymore.

Besides, Clay didn't fuck where he lived. That was the best way to avoid getting tied down or giving anyone leverage over you.

Give him an hour and he could rationalize it to himself. Right now, he just didn't want to see Grade put through a wall.

After a second, Ezra made a disgusted sound and let go. Grade slid down the wall, staggered, and caught his balance. He rubbed his neck as he shifted to the side.

"How the hell are you so calm?" Ezra asked. "The whole idea of us getting this lanky streak of piss in was so we could deny Buchanan had been killed on our patch. Now, not only did he get shot in the bathroom of my bar—on his first pickup from us—we cut the fucker up and put him in a van. We can't buy our way out of this. Fisher is going to want to make an example of us. It doesn't matter whether I piss off Janet or not. My kids are going to grow up without a dad either way."

There were a lot of ways to say the wrong thing right now. Clay could feel all of them rattling around behind his teeth.

My dad was around, and look how I turned out.

All this "we" and "us" is not how I remember it going down. That was all "you" and "I."

It always matters if you piss off Janet; that shit flows downhill.

All of that was true, and none of it would help. Clay pushed his hair back from his face, the curls damp and matted from a long night of fuckups that weren't his. He twisted it into a knot at the back of his skull as he looked at Grade.

"We blame him?" he said. Cute was all well and good, but Clay's own ass was always his first priority. And besides, he'd not have to see whatever happened. That would make it easier. He did feel bad enough to shrug an apology Grade's way as he tapped the nails into his coffin. "Guy goes around cutting up corpses all day every day—"

Grade bristled.

"It's not a hobby," he said. "I don't have a spine room that I show off on TikTok. It's just a job like—"

Ezra reached out and mashed a "shhh" finger against Grade's mouth. "Shut up," he said. "And trust me, everyone thinks you're a creepy little bastard. They'll believe the worst of you. And I know where your sister works, remember, so you'll play along."

For a second, something hard flickered through Grade's pretty eyes. It was there and gone in a flash, so quickly that Clay almost missed it. Most people probably did, but there was something nasty under all that precision and practicality. It wasn't going to help him, though.

Grade reached up and pushed Ezra's hand away from his face. He wiped the heel of his hand over his mouth.

"What if I get it back?" he said. "The van. The corpse."

Ezra pat-slapped Grade's cheek. "Nice thought," he said, the condescension thick as molasses. "But whoever has it obviously already knows what happened."

"So?" Grade asked. His eyes flicked to Clay for a second and then back to Ezra. "I know lots of things that happened in LA. So do the cops. Doesn't matter if they can't prove it."

Ezra shook his head and turned away. He walked over to the railing and leaned on it as he stared into the gray dawn light across the garden. The tattooed wings that covered his back flexed as he tensed his hands around the varnished handrail.

With Ezra's attention elsewhere, Grade shifted his weight restlessly from one foot to the other as he glanced briefly toward

Clay's car. The calculation was obvious on his face. Could he make it?

Clay dropped a hand on his shoulder and squeezed. He shook his head "no" and didn't relax his grip until Grade grimaced and slouched back into position against the wall. He stuck his hands in his pockets, knuckles sharp under the material, and bounced his heel nervously.

"It ain't the police I'm worried about," Ezra said. If it had occurred to him to worry about what Grade would do behind his back, it didn't show. Sometimes Clay wasn't sure if Ezra trusted him or was just that much of an arrogant dick.

Probably the "dick" thing. Yeah. For Ezra, that made sense.

Clay chewed on the ball of his thumb absently as he looked at Grade. Then he shrugged.

"What's the difference, though?" he said.

Ezra looked around at him and raised his eyebrows. He mugged an exaggerated thoughtful expression. "Um, I guess, off the top of my head, Fisher has a reputation for taking people that piss him off out on his boat to use as chum," he said, the words sharp enough to bite by the end of the sentence. "I'm no fan of the cops round here, but worst-case scenario, all they're going to do is take me down some dirt road, shoot me, and blame immigrants. At least there's no drama involved."

"And how often do they give a fuck?" Clay asked.

"Fisher or the cops?" Ezra asked.

"Yep," Clay said. He pointed a finger at Grade and mouthed "stay" before he walked over to lean back against the railing next to Ezra. "Look, the last thing Fisher wants is a war. It won't take him long to fuck us up—"

"Might take longer than he thinks," Ezra said.

"It won't," Clay said. "It's still time and money that Fisher could use to… the hell if I know what super-rich gangsters do for fun."

It was Grade who answered. "Same thing as the rest of us," he said. "Just in nicer rooms."

Ezra snorted as he turned around to look at Grade. "And you'd know?" he said. "What, you some LA kingpin's toy boy on the side?"

Grade twisted his mouth into a wry smile. "I wish," he said. "I wouldn't have had to come back here if ass was what I was selling. No, but you don't pay LA rent by getting rid of poor people's problems for them."

Fair enough. Clay caught Grade's gaze and held it. "Fucking then," he said, accent thick and lazy on the word. Same way he liked to do it. "On nice sheets."

For a second he didn't get any reaction to that. Then Grade swallowed hard, licked his lips, and looked down for a second. Clay grinned briefly with satisfaction. It was hardly the time, but good to know he still had it in the tank.

"Or," Ezra said, either missing or ignoring the subtext there, "maybe Fisher's idea of a good time is cutting bits off people to feed his pet shark. You think of that?"

Clay shrugged.

"Still cheaper ways to do it," he said. "If we give Fisher a way to ignore this—maybe a little something extra to sweeten the deal—he'd be an idiot not to take it."

"Maybe," Ezra said. He nodded at Grade. "And just so I'm clear, why isn't blaming this skinny asshole still on the table?"

"It is," Clay said. "But we serve him up to Fisher, we still have to admit we let his bagman get killed and his body desecrated on our turf. That's not exactly going to fill him with confidence about our ability to keep things tight. Buchanan just disappears—well, it sounds like that worked out well enough for Pulaski Senior. It might be enough to stop him writing us off completely."

For a second, nobody said anything as Ezra thought his options through. He didn't seem that pleased with any of them, but the flicker of light in a window upstairs distracted him before he could come up with any alternative.

"Daaaaaaaaaaaaaaaddy," a little girl's voice whined, snotty and drawn out. "It happened again."

"Fuck," Ezra muttered between tight lips. He jabbed a finger at Grade. "I need to go change some sheets, so I don't have time to deal with you right now. That means you get a chance to fix your mess. Buchanan's next stop was Sterling, in two days. You've got until someone calls me asking how Buchanan was when he left here to find the corpse and get rid of it. Got it?"

It turned out that Grade would be shit at poker. His relief at the reprieve was obvious on his face as he jerked his chin down in a quick nod of agreement.

"Got it," he said. "I'll make this right."

"Yeah, one way or another. And just in case you think you're smart," Ezra said. He turned to Clay. "You? Keep him close. I don't want to have to chase down… three, for god's sake, *three* different fuckers to throw to Fisher's sharks before he gets to me. So cometh the day, cometh the chum."

Clay screwed up his face. "I thought you wanted me to find TJ."

"Yeah, well," Ezra said. "Multi-task."

He stalked into the house, caught his daughter up just before she let herself out, and kicked the door shut behind him.

"C'mon. Sweetheart, c'mon," he said on the other side of the door, his voice fading as he headed down the hall. "It's some piss, that's all. I don't give a fuck. You think Daddy's never pissed himself? Don't cry."

That left two.

They stared at each other for a moment. Grade straightened his shirt with a fussy tug as he frowned at Clay.

"I'm not going anywhere," Grade said. "For the record. So if you've got somewhere else to be, don't worry about babysitting duty."

Clay stayed where he was, legs stretched out in front of him and thumbs hooked into the pockets of his jeans. He sucked a breath in through his teeth and shook his head.

"Nice try. Thing is, that sounds like what someone planning to make a run for it the minute I turn *would* say," Clay pointed out. "And I didn't put my ass on the line for you to hang me out to dry."

Grade glared at him. "You wanted to frame me for murder," he pointed out.

"As a last resort," Clay said as he finally pushed himself upright. He hooked his keys out of his pocket and idly spun them around his finger. "Besides, I'm your ride. You aren't going anywhere without me."

# DIRTY WORK

# CHAPTER FIVE

**IT HAD BEEN** a nice car once. Grade couldn't tell how long ago that was. The back roads around here did a number on "nice" cars. The potholes took out the suspension, and gravel wrecked the paint job. It wasn't a junker yet, but the resale value had clearly tanked.

The inside was clean enough, and it smelled of pine air freshener and a dark undernote of tobacco. The source of that was obvious as Clay took one hand off the wheel to light a cigarette. Shadows played over his cheekbone and temple as the flame flickered and jolted with the car; it caught threads of blond shot through his light brown hair.

"That's bad for you, you know," Grade said. He regretted it immediately. There were plenty of people he cared about out there making bad decisions; he didn't need to find anyone new to state the obvious to.

Clay shrugged as he let the flame gutter out on his lighter and tossed it into the center panel.

"How many people in our line of work do you know that live long enough to die of lung cancer?" he asked as he rolled the window down and hung his arm out. The night air blasted through the car, warm and oily from the road. "It's a young man's game."

Grade turned his head to look at Clay. He raised his eyebrows but didn't say anything. He didn't have to. After a second, Clay snorted. He flicked the butt of the cigarette with his thumb, and spark and ash sprayed out like a low-rent rainbow.

"I'm thirty-five," Clay said. "You want to give me funny looks, you need to wait another five years.... and be a bit less dependent on my good will."

That was a fair point.

Grade slouched down in his seat. He had a choice of what to watch, the nervous jiggle of his knee as he bounced his heel or the view out the dusty windshield of the dawn as it broke over the scabby outskirts of Sweeny.

A long stretch of broken, pot-holed road, the markings faded and worn off the concrete. The gas station that had been on its last legs when Grade last lived here had given up the ghost, the forecourt empty and the station's windows bricked up. Weeds grew out of the foundation and crawled up the side of the building. A poster, just about legible through the age-scratched plastic, promised the best BBQ in town.

That had always been a lie.

Along the side of the road, set on lots cut out of the tree line, there were run-down shacks and slightly better-condition trailers. Pickups sat on most of the drives. The difference was if they had wheels or were up on blocks.

This wasn't the part of town that Grade had grown up in. He came from the shithole on the other side. Mining vs. loggers. No one had won that one.

Well, no one in town had. The companies involved had come out pretty loaded at the end of the day.

"Fucking Sweeny," Grade said as he tilted his head back and closed his eyes.

Clay chuckled, a sound full of lazy humor. "Think you're too good for us, City Boy?"

"For this town? Yeah," Grade said. He opened one eye to look over at Clay as he asked. "You don't?"

There was a pause as Clay lifted his hand to his mouth and put the cigarette between his lips. The end of it glowed dully as he flicked the indicator on and spun the wheel to take the hairpin turn onto the main road into town.

"People find their own level," Clay said as he plucked the cigarette from his mouth. He stubbed it out against the side of the car and flicked the butt toward the scrub that lined the edge of the road. "I guess Sweeny is mine. It could be worse."

"Yeah, that just means you've not been here long enough," Grade grumbled.

The words escaped before he thought better of it. He bit the end of his tongue in annoyance at himself. Clay wasn't his friend or his peer, and Grade needed to remember that. He didn't *need* to share his thoughts on the man's health, habits, or habitat. It wasn't like he had back in LA. Plenty of his clients behaved badly—to themselves and others—and Grade kept his opinion of them to himself.

Except when it involved invoicing, of course,

"It's treated me well enough," Clay said. He paused as they both watched the picked-over carcass of the old processing tower come up on the left. The scaffolding listed, and the corrugated iron siding had warped and rusted into holes and crevices. Clay hung one hand over the steering wheel, fingers relaxed, and shrugged as he glanced at Grade. "What? I was never gonna be a miner, and there's still plenty of demand for men like me."

It was the perfect time for Grade to shut his mouth. So, of course, he didn't.

"People need crime done in LA too," Grade said. "And they also have Korean BBQ and gay bars. So..."

"Good to know," Clay said.

He left it at that. Which was good. Grade definitely hadn't just brought that up because he wanted Clay to know he was gay.

*"Why did you, then?"* the snotty mental voice that always sounded a bit like his sister asked.

It was a good question. The answer was that Grade's taste in men had always run to tattooed and bad news. He did not make good choices, and he preferred it that way. But this wasn't the time or the place. Grade needed to find his van, save his ass, and build up enough of a nest egg to fund a second start in the big to middling city. He'd prefer LA, but at this point, he'd work with anything on the West Coast. And there would be *plenty* of unreliable, untrustworthy men to fuck him *and* his life up out there.

He didn't need anything to be more complicated right now. And maybe Clay was straight, or just not interested. Not everyone was into high-strung nerds.

Grade bounced his knee in silence as they drove into Sweeny with the dawn. Dusty old buildings and more storefronts boarded up than there had been when he left. Half of the big old redbrick buildings were empty too, doors sealed and windows bricked up. The bank had left with the mining company, and the rest of the town had been trickling out after it ever since.

"Where are we going, anyhow?" Clay asked as he braked at the crosswalk to let an old woman hobble over the road, her weight braced on her walker. "Not like you can go to the cops and report that someone stole the corpse you chopped up."

"I used a saw," Grade said. He stretched his arm over Clay's chest and indicated the street corner ahead of them. "Turn there. Stop at the pink house with the muscle car outside."

Clay took the corner tight and waved what could have been an apology or a fuck off at the wrecked-looking man in the Toyota with a primer-red hood. He cruised past the back lots of the store and pulled up in front of the black-topped purple Dodge.

"Nice car," Clay said dryly. "Yours?"

"No," Grade said as he popped the seat belt and scrambled out of the car. He bent down to look at Clay through the door. "Wait here. I'll not be long."

He slammed the door shut and headed inside.

§

Dory's shift must have run over.

She was dressed for the couch in sweats and a crop top as she made sloppy sandwiches in the small kitchen, but her arms were covered in body glitter, and her hair was still pulled up into a high ponytail. The full face of makeup she had on looked odd in the morning. It had been put on under fluorescents, and the shades were just a bit off under natural light.

She looked up from the generous spread of special no-nut peanut butter. Some people would have wasted time on "relieved." Dory skipped that and went straight to exasperated.

"Where have you been?" she asked, her free hand propped on her hip and butter knife held loosely in the other as she gestured with it. "It's after six. You were supposed to sort Cody's lunch and take him to school and what happened to your forehead?"

Grade paused mid-step. He reached up to touch his forehead, but caught himself before he poked the bruise. "You look like mom when you do that," he said instead.

"I do… Don't you try and start a fight with me," Dory snapped. She slapped the knife down on the cutting board and crossed her arms. Her foot tapped on the floor. "Cody looks up to you. If you let him down, he could end up with inauthentic attachment problems."

"That sounds made up."

"Well, it *isn't*. Shows what you know."

Grade cut around the table and grabbed Dory's backpack from the hook on the door. He waved it at her.,

"Is your phone in here?"

She narrowed her eyes. "Why? And are you trying to change the subject?"

"I gave him a fifty," Grade said. "And I want to know where your phone is."

"What do you mean you gave him a fifty?" Dory said. "He's twelve. Where do you think he's getting his lunch? DoorDash?"

"If he wants," Grade said. "It's his money."

"He's *twelve*," Dory repeated. "That means he gets a packed lunch, not hookers and blow money."

Grade pulled the top of the bag open and stuck his arm in. "Even in Sweeny, I don't think fifty is going to get you both. He'll have to pick his vice."

Dory made an aggrieved noise and stamped her foot. You can't buy his love. If you want to be in his life, you'll have to show up for him. And stop that! I didn't say you could look in there."

"You didn't say I couldn't."

"Give me my bag."

"Give me your phone."

They both glared at each other over the table for a second. Then Dory smirked and crossed her arms, weight shifted over onto one foot.

"My diaphragm is in there," she said, little-sister smug.

Grade looked at the bag and then at her. He shrugged. "What's it going to do? Crawl out and bite me?" he asked. "Is it an attack diaphragm? Does it have teeth? Do you call it Growler?"

Despite her mood, the corner of Dory's mouth quirked up; the dimple they shared suddenly hinted at under the heavy powder.

"I mean, I do *now*," she said. "*Obviously*. God, you're terrible at being a brother. My phone's in the side pocket. It's locked, though. So if you want to use it, you're going to have to tell me what you want it for."

She singsonged the last three words and turned away to ostentatiously go back to making the sandwiches. Grade made a face at her. It was hard not to fall into old habits, even with the current situation and his literal deadline. He unzipped the pocket and pulled out a glitter-pink phone and a handful of bright yellow condoms.

"They're for you," Dory said over her shoulder. "The Chicken is giving them away for free. Pandemic measure. Glove up against Covid."

"I don't think condoms will help," Grade said. "My penis isn't out there touching stuff."

Dory twisted at the waist so he could appreciate the saccharine-sweet smile she gave him over her shoulder. "Maybe yours isn't," she said. "Some people have game."

"Some people. Not whoever is running around with Sinestro dick," Grade said as he stuffed the condoms back into the bag.

Dory muttered "nerd" under her breath, but he ignored that. He tapped the screen to wake it up. Dory's lock screen was an old photo of them with their Dad, in the original Dodge. Before things went to shit. Grade managed not to comment as he tapped in her birthday—wrong guess. Cody's birthday was his next try, but that was wrong as well. Grade stopped for a second and stared at the old photo of their Dad, his arms slung around their shoulders as they squeezed up together to look out the passenger side window. The sinking feeling in his stomach made him hope he was wrong, but he tapped the date in anyhow—twelfth of March, 2012. The lock screen slid out of the way, and Grade made a frustrated sound in his throat. "Shit, Dory. Are you ever going to stop picking at it?"

Her back was turned to him again. She just shrugged as she slapped the pieces of bread together and sliced them in perfect triangles. The knife cut into the board audibly.

"No."

Grade opened his mouth to argue. All the old faithfuls were there, ready to throw at her head. If Dad wasn't dead, then he'd just run out on them. People in real life didn't get amnesia and disappear, and they weren't kidnapped and held for a decade. They died, or they left. Pick one. Except he'd said it all before, and he'd managed to hurt Dory's feelings a few times, but he'd never convinced her. At the end of the day, reality didn't matter.

Dad coming home was her LA.

"I'm not the boss of you," he admitted as he looked down at the phone. The screens slid to the side under his thumb as he hunted through a hundred random app downloads for the one he wanted.

"So?" Dory said, her voice pitched to pierce. "Are you going to tell me why you were out all night? Did you blow off your family 'cause you got lucky? That's pretty shitty for my only brother."

Grade was about to shoot her down, but he didn't get the chance.

"I don't know how lucky he was," Clay said. He leaned against the back door, shoulder propped against the frame, and gave Dory a slow, suggestive smile. "I think I got the better end of that deal."

Dory stared at him for a second. "Uh-huh," she said. Then she sidled around the table and grabbed Grade's arm. She hissed in his ear, "Can I have a fucking word?"

There it was. Grade tapped the tracking app with his thumb. It opened up and then stalled as it started to update something.

"No," he told Dory. "It was work, OK?"

Dory let go of his arm and punched him in the shoulder instead. She still knew how to throw a punch.

"You promised that you wouldn't bring that around Cody," she hissed. "I don't want him involved in anything shady."

Grade rubbed his arm. "I didn't. He wasn't there," he said and waved the phone at her. "I'm going to need to borrow your phone."

"What? No," she said.

"Why?" Clay asked.

The interruption caught Grade off guard. He had been low-key aware of Clay all night—for reasons that were smart and, ah, not so much—but the familiarity of bickering with Dory had distracted him. He'd almost forgotten Clay was there.

"I asked him that," Dory said, prickly at the offense of it. "He wouldn't tell me."

Clay smiled, slow and crooked, as he tucked his hand into the pocket of his jeans. The battered denim slouched low around his lean waist.

"I've got a bit more leverage," he said. "Your brother wants to keep me… sweet."

He winked at Dory. She frowned at him.

"I know you," she said. "I've seen you at the Chicken, collecting the money from my boss. He's scared of you."

Clay's smile didn't slip. "Yeah, well, he's supposed to be," he said.

"My van was stolen," Grade said. "I need to get it back."

"You're going to call in a favor?" Clay asked. "I could have lent you my phone for that."

Dory rolled her eyes. "He doesn't do favors," she said. "It's cash or credit only with him. Paid up front."

"Yeah, well, we all saw how much favors helped Dad," Grade muttered.

He'd meant her to hear it. Yet he still regretted that she had when he saw the hurt flash over her face. Before he could work out how to apologize, without using the words "I'm sorry," the door behind swung open and hit him in the hip.

"Mom?" Cody said as he stuck his head into the kitchen. His hair was still patchy blue from a misjudged attempt to dye it with Kool-Aid. "Did you make me anything for lunch?"

Grade nudged the door back into Cody. "Hey. I gave you fifty bucks for your lunch."

Cody pushed back against the door and craned his neck so he could see Grade. He gave a gap-toothed grin.

"Yeah," he said. "And if I get a packed lunch instead, I'm fifty bucks up."

Clay snorted, and Cody looked over at the door. He gaped in surprise for a second and then recovered quickly.

"Oh, hey," he said, shoving the door open with his crutch to shuffle into the kitchen. "Hi. I'm Cody. Are you Uncle Grade's boyfriend?"

"No" came from Grade and Dory at the same moment.

The amused "Maybe" came from Clay as he grinned at Cody. "I'm Clay. Pleased to meet you."

"Yeah," Cody said. "Wow! Your ink is sick. It's really—"

"That's enough," Dory interrupted him. She grabbed his shoulders and pushed him out into the hall. "Go get dressed. I'm taking you to school."

"But Uncle Grade can..." Cody whined in protest as the door swung shut behind both of them.

"No," Dory said, her voice muffled by the door. "I'm going to embarrass you in front of all your friends. Now go. Get dressed. And not the Magneto T-shirt. I want people to think you own more than one outfit!"

While they argued, Grade shifted his attention back to Clay again. He grimaced a vague "sorry about my family" smile at him and held Dory's phone up.

"I left my phone in the car," he said. "Dory has access to my location services, so..."

Clay pulled a dubious face. "Phone's going to be the first thing they throw out of the car, though."

"It was in the glove box," Grade said. "So with any luck, it will have taken them a while to find it. Then at least we'll know what direction they went in."

He swiped down the list of Dory's contacts—friends, family, and exes—until he reached his name. The last time she'd checked on him, apparently, had been two days ago. Probably to see if he'd been nearly home with the takeout.

He thumbed the screen down and waited for it to update.

"Why was your phone in the glove box?" Clay asked.

Grade shifted to the side as the kitchen door swung open again as Dory came back in. "It's safest. Ideally, your phone shouldn't be visible when you're driving. Even looking to see what a notification is can distract you from the road long enough for an accident."

"He might be a criminal," Dory said to Clay, her voice dry. "But he's very law-abiding."

Grade glanced up from the phone. "I get stopped by the cops with a bag of—"

Dory snapped her fingers at him and pointed up at the ceiling, her face screwed up in an expression of exaggerated irritation.

"Laundry—" Grade edited himself with. "Happy?" he mouthed at Dory. "—in the back of the van, I'll get charged with a lot worse than a traffic violation. So I drive safely—and when my van gets jacked, I can find it."

Clay pushed himself off the door and straightened up.

"Where?" he said.

Grade slid his fingers over the screen to zoom in on the icon that represented his car.

"Out of town," he said. The dirt roads up that way were lucky to have a number, never mind a name. "Up near the hunting camps."

"Let's go, then," Clay said as he tilted his head to the door. "As much fun as meeting your family has been, we're still up against the clock."

He nodded to Dory, "See you at work," and headed out the door.

Grade went to follow him, but Dory grabbed his arm first. Her nails dug into his forearm through his shirt.

"Whatever this is, and I don't want to know," she said. Ignorance was safety. Grade hadn't learned that lesson on his own. "Is there any chance it's going to come back on us? Mum and me? Cody?"

She waited.

There were a lot of good things in LA. Grade counted them instead of sheep sometimes when he couldn't sleep. In the top five was that he didn't have anyone he loved there. Friends, acquaintances, roommates. People he knew, but no one that could be used against him.

"No," Grade lied. "I promise. If I can't fix it, it's all on me."

Dory let go of his arm. She folded her arms as she stepped back.

"Again?"

He hesitated for a second and then reached into his jacket. He pulled out the fee Ezra had paid for the clean-up job and pushed it into her hands.

"If anything happens..."

"What?" she snapped as she shoved the money back at him. "You die and I send Cody to med school on... what... five grand?"

"Six, and just take it." Grade shoved it into a cupboard and slammed the door. "Nothing is going to happen, but I'll be out of touch for a couple of days. If anything comes up, you've got some cash to deal with it."

He left before she could argue with him anymore.

# DIRTY WORK

# CHAPTER SIX

**CLAY PULLED IN** at the Bear Pit.

It had started out life as a gas station, but the owners had added more strings to their bow as the years went on. Now it sold hunting gear, dehydrated rations, ammo, and booze—everything a hunter who wanted to make the most of the two weeks they'd paid five grand for could want. The white paint had faded off the clapboard walls, leaving them gray and weathered. Old bow-hunting targets and beer posters were roughly plastered over the walls.

There was a single pump outside. It wasn't in use.

"No sign of your van," Clay said. "Does the app have a hot-and-cold setting?"

Grade shook his head. "No," he said, as he turned his sister's phone off. Glitter suspended in blue gel slurped across the back of the case as he tucked it into his jeans. "We're in the circle, but I think that's as close as it is going to get."

He stared at the Pit for a second, then visibly shook off whatever was on his mind and got out of the car. The morning sun picked out red in his hair as he headed away from the car, only to stop and look back curiously at Clay. He waved his hand toward the Pit in a mute "you coming?" and raised his eyebrows.

Clay weighed his options as he studied Grade through the windshield. The filter of grime gave a patina of morning-after-the-night-before to the squeaky-clean frat boy look, and that had its appeal. This was work, though, so Clay couldn't just follow his cock after a lean ass and a smart mouth. Not blindly, anyhow.

It could be a wild goose chase. Grade had every reason in the world to buy time going here, there, and everywhere while he tried to come up with a way out of this. He didn't owe Ezra anything, unlike Clay.

But what the hell. It was a nice ass, and TJ could wait. The kid was hardly a criminal genius; he wasn't going to get far.

Clay turned the engine off and got out of the car. He stretched lazily and didn't miss that Grade eyes dropped to where his shirt crawled up to flash a lean slice of taut skin. Or the quick, nervy way he licked his lips as he looked away.

Served him right. Thirty-five wasn't so old that Clay couldn't make someone's cock hard at the worst possible time. It was really going to suck if he had to serve Grade up to the Catfish Mafia. Or... *not* suck.

"You take a look around the back and see if you can find anything," he said.

"Sure you trust me not to run off?" Grade asked sourly.

Clay could lie, he supposed, but what would be the point? It wasn't like Grade had forgotten the stakes of this particular scavenger hunt, and Clay knew what role he'd end up playing. He didn't have to like it, but... it still had to be done.

"I know where your sister lives," Clay pointed out, his voice level and matter-of-fact. "And you seem to like her, so... I'm pretty sure you're not going anywhere."

He shrugged. It wasn't a personal threat—just business—but it was still a threat.

Grade grimaced and looked away.

"I could do with a coffee," he said, his voice so dry it puckered. "Think I could get an oatmilk latte?"

Clay laughed and headed inside.

§

The Pit didn't have oat milk. It did have sides of warmed-over ribs.

Clay handed over a dollar for two and stripped the meat off the bone as he waited for the heavyset man behind the till to pour out two black coffees. It wasn't *good*, but the smoky, too-sweet sauce and fatty meat still hit the spot. He might regret it later, but he might be drunk later, so what the hell.

He'd just started on the second rib when the clerk slid the cups across the counter in a cardboard holder.

"Six dollars," the man said.

"Seriously?" Clay said through a mouthful of rib, his hand tucked into his back pocket to retrieve his wallet. "I could get Starbucks for that."

The man scratched his eyebrow. "So go to Starbucks," he said and jerked his thumb toward the door. "It's twenty minutes down the road."

And people called Clay a crook.

Clay pulled his wallet out and peeled off a ten. He folded it between his greasy fingers and held it out.

"You want change?" the clerk asked, without altering his slack expression.

Clay squinted at him for a second. When the dour look on the man's face didn't crack, he dropped the rib onto a napkin and wiped his mouth on the back of his hand.

"What is this, Roux 21?" he asked. Maybe Grade's bitterness about Sweeny had gotten to him more than he thought. It had been years since he'd thought about his favorite restaurant back in Baton Rouge, not since he'd been there after he finished his last tour. "Give me my money."

He stuck his hand out and wriggled his fingers. The clerk grunted, slapped the till open, and pulled the crumpled notes out to count pointedly into Clay's palm.

"You seen a couple of guys in a laundry van around here?" Clay asked as he slid the notes into the back of his wallet. "They'd have been here just before dawn. And I tip better for good intel than for bad coffee."

The clerk glanced over Clay's shoulder. Clay turned.

TJ was still dressed in the clothes he'd had on the night before, but his T-shirt was damp where he'd tried to scrub the bloodstains out. It hadn't worked. Clay could have told him that, but some things you had to learn on your own.

The color drained from his face as he stared at Clay. Lucky enough, he'd just used the toilet or his jeans would have stained too.

"Now that," Clay said as he pulled a fifty out of his wallet and handed it back over his shoulder. The clerk coughed, a dry little hitch of discomfort, but didn't hesitate to snag the note. "is what I call convenient. TJ. Been looking for you."

Interesting fact that Clay had picked up over the years: when the shit hit the fan, it didn't matter if someone was brilliant or an idiot. Not for Clay, anyhow. A smartass like Grade could run all the angles before he made a move, while a moron like TJ just reacted while his brain was still running the loading screen. Yet no matter how many steps it took to get there, by the time the decision tree got as far as Clay, there were only three routes left.

Fight, flight, or "we can figure this out."

That was the only part Clay had to care about.

"Don't make me chase you," Clay warned. "I just ate."

TJ sucked in a ragged, uneven breath, and then he bolted, the wet soles of his trainers squeaky on the tiled floor as he headed toward the back of the store.

"Fuck me," Clay sighed.

He tossed the half-eaten rib down on the counter and went after TJ. The skinny man grabbed one of the shelves and shoved it over. Cans of "human grade" stew and slippery plastic sleeves of jerky spilled over the floor as the metal stand crashed down. Clay cursed under his breath as he brought his foot down on a can and nearly went on his ass.

"Not doing yourself any favors," he growled as he caught himself.

"Leave me alone!" TJ yelled back at him. He shouldered the door open into the back room and slammed it behind him. The click of a lock as it slid into place made Clay swear through clenched teeth.

He turned as he reached the door, dipped at the waist, and hit it shoulder first. It held for a moment, just long enough for Clay to decide he was going to kill the clerk to keep this embarrassing clusterfuck under wraps. Then the bolt ripped out of the frame and the door slammed open. It smacked back into the wall, Clay half fell through it, and the clerk got to live another day.

Probably. The door swung shut again behind Clay as he got his bearings.

The storeroom was dark and smelled like old blood and ammo. Clay reached out to grope along the wall for the switch. He flicked it on, and the overhead lights audibly crackled to life with a dim yellow glow. Enough to illuminate TJ at the other end of the room, his face set in a panicked mask and a desert camo X-Bolt cocked to his shoulder.

"I t-t-told you to leave me alone," TJ stuttered as his finger trembled on the trigger. "You should have... have listened."

Clay exhaled slowly. Everything slowed down as he focused on the gun Some people tensed up when they were threatened, but to Clay it always felt easy and familiar. He licked his lips, mouth dry, and then grinned at TJ.

"You ain't the first to say that," he said. "You won't be the last."

TJ pressed his lips together in a hard line as he tilted the muzzle of the gun up so it pointed right at Clay's head.

"Might be," he said.

There was something wrong with the thin sliver of anticipation that caught in the back of Clay's throat. It felt a bit like the moment before someone touched his cock, but he knew they were going to, so he'd not needed the army shrink to point that out. Thing was, that didn't make it any less fun.

He stepped forward, and his stomach tightened. "Yeah, don't think so," he said. "You're shit scared, TJ. Your hands are shaking. If there was any piss left in you, then you've managed to squeeze it out. Did you load that? Did you check if it was loaded? 'Cause it ain't."

The corner of TJ's mouth trembled as he stared at Clay. Then he jerked the gun to the side and fired. The bullet smacked into the wall a few inches from Clay's head, and the echo of the gunshot bounced around the storeroom. In the store outside, someone yelled. Clay laughed, a breathless whoop of glee, and bounced on the balls of his feet.

"Yeah! Wow. Called my bluff," he said. "Remind me never to play poker with you."

"I grew up hunting," TJ said. "I know how to load a rifle and how to… What the fuck's so funny? I could kill you. That's what you're here to do to me, right? So why shouldn't I?"

Clay swayed to one side and the other to see how well TJ tracked him. "You should," he said. "It'd be the smart call."

TJ shifted his grip on the gun. "You're crazy."

Clay held up one finger. "Unstable," he corrected him. "It's… different medication, mostly. Don't worry about it."

He nudged one foot forward and to the side, toward the stack of plastic-wrapped cardboard boxes in the middle of the room. It wouldn't provide much cover. At this range, the X-Bolt would punch a bullet right through the boxes and the—he glanced sidelong at the labels—franks and beans inside. It would work as a bluff, though.

The X-Bolt was a nice gun, but it wasn't designed for close combat.

"They said you'd blame me," TJ muttered to himself. His finger flexed against the trigger, barely enough to dent the skin, but it still made a thrill prickle the back of Clay's neck. He focused on that and filed the words away to deal with later. "That I'd go down for it, but I ain't gonna—"

The door to the storeroom swung open.

"Someone shot Judd," Grade said after a beat. Observant little bastard. Clay hadn't gotten the name, and he'd talked to the man. Grade's voice stayed even and calm as he came into the room. "Everything OK in here?"

The muzzle of the gun switched between Grade and Clay as TJ tried to decide what to do. He backed up until his heels hit the wall behind him. The jolt made him fumble the gun briefly, long enough to make the skin over Clay's shoulders tighten uncomfortably.

*His* potential death was all in good fun, but not so much when someone else was involved.

"All good with me," Clay said. He snapped his fingers to pull TJ's attention back to him. "Hey. Pay attention. You're going to have to shoot one of us, right? Him or me. Who's it going to be?"

TJ clenched his jaw and swallowed convulsively. He gestured with the gun. "Go stand n-n-next to him."

"No," Clay said. He took a step forward. "Him or me, TJ. Pick a poison. We ain't got all day."

"What's wrong with you!" TJ demanded. Sweat dripped down his face as he edged along the wall to try and keep the same distance between them. "What the *fuck* is your problem?"

"Oh, we don't have the time for that," Clay said. His voice picked up intensity. "C'mon, TJ. You've done it before. What are you waiting on?"

Grade cleared his throat. "Or?" he said. "He could put the gun down? Maybe? Murder isn't always the answer."

"That's rich," Clay said. "Coming from someone in your line of work. How are you going to get back to LA with that sort of attitude, City Boy?"

Out of the corner of his eye, he saw Grade shoot him a dirty look.

"Sometimes it's the answer," he said. "Doesn't have to be today. Right, TJ?"

"Uh-huh," Clay said. "TJ promised me he was going to shoot someone. You're not going to blue ball me now, right, TJ?"

TJ's chest rose and fell rapidly as his eyes darted back and forth between the two of them. Then he set his jaw and jerked the gun toward Clay. He squeezed his eyes closed as he pulled the trigger.

Shit.

"Clay!" Grade yelled as he stepped forward.

Clay threw himself to the side, into the stack of boxes. The bullet clipped the side of his head, traced a line of heat from his ear back through his hair. For a *second*, it occurred to him that it might not have missed. He could be dead, stuck in the lag before the news reached his brain stem.

Blood dripped onto the back of his head, and he sucked in a quick ragged breath.

Apparently not. What the hell, then. Clay braced his elbow on the boxes, shoved himself back upright, and headed for TJ.

TJ made a guttural, panicked noise as he tried to bring the gun back into position. But the X-Bolt was a long-range rifle, and while the 21-foot rule was mostly just used to justify deadly force, four feet was too close to fend off someone with a rifle.

Even if you used it as a club.

Clay blocked the wild swing of the rifle with one forearm, a dull thud of impact as the narrow barrel smacked into muscle, and tackled TJ.

He slammed the dissident back into the rocks and, as the sand slid under their feet, wrenched the rifle out of his hands.

He tossed it to Ezra…

No.

He didn't. They weren't in Afghanistan and it was Grade who, just about, caught the weapon and cradled it awkwardly.

Clay shook his head. It was still ringing. That didn't help. He grabbed a handful of—*dusty camo, Kevlar straps*—old Willie Nelson T-shirt and hauled TJ off the wall. The lanky man dangled from his own shirt, sleeves rucked up under his armpits and snot on his upper lip.

"You were supposed to shoot at him," he said as he jerked his head toward Grade. "You idiot."

He let go of TJ, who staggered as he landed back on his feet. Before he could do anything, Clay drew his fist back and coldcocked him across the jaw. TJ stumbled backward, mouth slack, and then his eyes rolled in different directions and he dropped.

"He was supposed to shoot me?" Grade said, his voice pitched up with indignation. "Why?"

Clay touched his forehead and brought his fingers away bloody. The confirmation of the injury made his brain register the dull throb of pain that bounced around his skull. That was great. He wiped his hands on his jeans.

"I don't like being shot?" he said. It seemed like that should be self-explanatory, even if not always 100 percent true. "And it's not like he'd have killed you, except by mistake. I just needed him to aim away from me for a second. By the way, didn't I tell you to stay outside?"

Grade hesitated for a second—obviously still fishing for a way to stay butt-hurt—but his survival instincts won out.

"I found the van," he said. "It's around the back of the store, next to the shower block. I guess my phone is still in it."

Clay wriggled a finger in his ear to try and pop the rattle of static out of his head. It didn't work. His offended ears rang, and the memory of hot sand and dusty tents kept encroaching on the sides of reality.

It was fine; it would pass—that old refrain.

"You OK?" Grade asked. He reached up and indicated his own head. "You're bleeding."

"It's just a head injury," Clay said. "It's not my first. Any sign of anyone else around?"

Grade shook his head.

"Well, that just opens up a load of new questions, doesn't it?' Clay said as he leaned down and grabbed the back of TJ's shirt. He dragged TJ's limp body behind him as he headed for the fire doors. "Let's get some answers."

# DIRTY WORK

# CHAPTER SEVEN

**GRADE WINCED AS** Clay smashed the side window of the van with a rock. At this point, it would probably be cheaper to pull out the customizations and get a new van rather than fix it. It still stung. His savings were going to be stripped back to pennies at this rate.

At least that was one thing he wouldn't have to worry about if he ended up as bait in a net.

Clay reached an arm into the van and popped the lock. He stepped back as the door swung open to let Grade have first crack at the mess. The glove box had been cracked open and emptied out, the first aid box upended and coins scattered over the floor. Someone had taken a box cutter to the seats and pulled out handfuls of sponge. The carpets had been pulled up too, and the metal underneath was grooved with deep, raw scrapes from a claw hammer.

A Russian drug dealer up in Frisco had a fondness for those *and* a bad aim. Grade had spackled over the marks he'd left in the walls of his apartment often enough.

The steering column had been cracked open too, and the radio ripped out.

"What were they looking for?" Grade asked.

"Maybe they thought you had money," Clay suggested.

Grade gave him an annoyed look. "If I had money, why would I still be here?" he asked.

Clay crossed his arms and leaned against the front of the van. He tilted his head to the side and pulled a thoughtful face.

"Maybe they thought you were an asshole."

That was more likely, but...

"In that case, they'd have pissed in it," Grade said.

He found his phone down the side of the driver's seat, jammed into the tracks. The screen came on when he tapped it, but it was locked. From the greasy fingerprints all over the screen, it looked like they'd tried to unlock it and guessed his code wrong enough times to brick the account. Grade stuck it into his back pocket—he could reset it later—and twisted around between the seats to crawl through the hatch into the back.

After this many years, it took a lot to make him retch. The smell in the back did. It wasn't the blood someone had tipped over the back like slurry, tacky under the soles of his shoes, but the pile of ripe puke in the corner. It smelled like rancid cheese. Grade grimaced and wished he'd grabbed the pot of wintergreen back out of the drinks holder.

He pressed the back of his hand to his nose and took a second to take stock. Once that was done, he made his way gingerly—just in case blood and bleach weren't all that was underfoot—to the back doors. The lock had been mangled with something, but he steadied himself against the sides of the van and gave it a kick. First time did nothing. The second time—hard enough that he felt the impact in his knee—it popped open.

Clay caught the doors before they could fly all the way back. He glanced past Grade into the back of the van.

"Anything out of place?" he deadpanned.

Grade rolled his eyes. "Ha, ha," he said. "Give me a hand?"

He stuck his out. Clay hesitated for a second and then took it, fingers tangled together and warm as Grade jumped down onto the gravel that covered the lot. For a second, he was very close to Clay, and he could smell sweat, blood, and cordite layered over whiskey. It caught in the back of Grade's throat and tickled under his skin. He thought about hanging onto Clay's hand, just to see what happened. He let go instead.

"Body's gone," he said as he stepped away. In the back of his head, he made a mental note to trash the shoes before he went back home. "Most of it."

Clay had started to say something. He stopped and gave Grade a dubious look.

"Most of it?"

Fair enough, Grade supposed. Sweeny wasn't his professional stomping grounds after all. There was no reason Clay would know the process.

"Fingers and teeth," he said. "I removed them back at The Slap. I learned that on day one. You don't want to be stuck at the dumpsite in the middle of the night doing impromptu dental work on a corpse. They didn't realize and left them behind."

Or have to drive back there because you forgot, but that wasn't something any of Grade's professional associates needed to know. Besides, everyone had a first day on the job. It wasn't like he'd not learned his lesson.

"Do you keep them?" Clay asked.

"Of course not," Grade said. A hint of mild offense sharpened his voice. "I'm not a serial killer. I burn them."

"Oh well, that's OK then." Clay climbed up onto the bumper of the van, arms slung over the doors for balance, and craned his neck to get a good look at the mess. "Any chance that the remains they got would be unidentifiable?"

Grade shook his head. "I doubt they'll have an open casket," he said. "But his mother would be able to pick him out of a line-up."

"Yeah, well, I wouldn't know what to do if the world didn't piss in my Cheerios," Clay said. He jumped back down, dusted his hands off, and turned to look at the wannabe shooter. TJ Hall lay on his side in the gravel, his hands tied behind him with repurposed straps cut from the boxes in the storeroom. Blood had dried around his mouth, and his eyes were closed as he tried to pretend he was still unconscious. Clay sighed and stalked over. He braced his foot against TJ's shoulder and gave him a shove. "When you're pretending to be unconscious, you moron, don't hold your breath."

After a brief hesitation, TJ ostentatiously exhaled.

This time when Clay's foot connected with him, it was definitely a kick.

TJ rolled over and tried to get to his feet. Hindered by his hands trussed together at the wrists, he managed to get awkwardly onto his knees; then Clay knocked him back down.

TJ curled into a ball in the expectation of more, his hands folded over his head.

The nudge of pity was unexpected. Grade supposed that whatever TJ was, he was also the guy who'd *not* shot him.

"Where's the body?" Grade asked.

Clay snorted as he leaned down and grabbed the neck of TJ's T-shirt. He dragged him up onto his feet and gave him a shake.

"Trust me, City Boy," he said. "Playing good cop is just going to confuse TJ. He's not used to that sort of thing. Isn't that right, TJ?"

TJ cleared his throat and spat a mixture of blood and saliva onto the ground.

"You a cop?" he asked suspiciously as he squinted at Grade.

Clay rolled his eyes. "I didn't hit you that hard, TJ. Try and get all three of those brain cells in line, yeah? Where's the body that was in the van?"

"I don't know what you mean," TJ said after a brief hesitation. He sniffed and ducked his head down to try and wipe his nose on his shoulder. "This ain't nothing to do with me."

Clay slapped him across the back of the head. "We don't have time for games," he said. "What did you do with the body? Answer the man."

Color flushed TJ's cheeks in slap-bright swatches of angry pink. He wrenched away from Clay.

"Or what?" he spat. "You're gonna kill me? Like that ain't already the plan?"

Clay's mouth folded into a dog's smile. He licked his lips and dragged TJ back in, his arm thrown over thin shoulders.

"Yeah," Clay admitted. His voice was still all honey and Southern charm, but it managed to be cold at the same time. "But let's be real. I don't have to make it quick."

He winked at TJ.

It had been obvious Clay was dangerous, but this was the first time he'd sent a chill of uneasy fear down Grade's back. It was probably unfortunate that gave it a straight run down to Grade's balls. He tried not to squirm in place as he took a shallow breath that felt hot and tight in his chest.

Worst taste in men.

"I... I ain't—" The warning whoop of a siren cut through the morning stillness, crude and loud. Everyone turned to look as the police cruiser turned around the side of the Pit and pulled up. The door opened, and a deputy climbed out. He stood with his hand rested casually on his gun as he looked at them for a second, then raised his free hand to gesture them over.

"Clerk called the cops," Clay said. He shook his head, more in disappointment than disgust.

"He did get shot," Grade pointed out. They'd left the clerk slumped on the floor of his own store, a wad of toilet paper pressed to the through-and-through in his thigh. "Most people think that you have to call 9-1-1 in that situation."

Clay snorted. "You've been in LA too long." He shoved TJ over to Grade. "Take care of him. I'll deal with this."

He leveled a finger at TJ's face in mute warning and then turned and sauntered across the lot to the waiting deputy. Grade rubbed his hands down his thighs and took a deep, nervous breath as he tried *very hard* not to think about the tacky layer of blood on the soles of his shoes or the bits and pieces of body still left in the back.

"I wouldn't worry," TJ said. He leaned back against the van and slid down into a crouch, his back braced against the black rim of the tire. "Cops around here consider kickbacks part of their salary."

"Don't you watch TV?" Grade asked. "You can't trust people to stay bought anymore. If it's not immunity on the table, it's their conscience."

TJ snorted and leaned his head back against the side of the van. His throat worked as he swallowed hard. "Yeah, well, Jones's conscience got buried with his career in Lexington."

It wasn't money that Clay offered. The baggie of white powder he produced from his jeans did the trick, though. After a glance around, Jones took it and made it disappear into his pocket.

That was a good sign. Grade was still fidgety with nerves, but he didn't think he'd do well in jail. He shifted his weight absently from one foot to the other and tried to think of something else. Anything else. Even if it broke his usual rules… and involved asking questions.

"Why didn't you kill him?" he asked.

TJ looked up at him. "What? You don't like him either?"

It was an easy in, but for some reason, Grade was reluctant to say no. Luckily enough, though, he didn't have to answer TJ's question.

"Why hesitate?" Grade pushed. "If you'd shot him, you could have been on the interstate by now. Halfway to the state line by the time Ezra realized he needed to stick someone else on your trail."

TJ pressed his lips together and looked down at his grubby knees. It looked like Grade wasn't going to get an answer, but just as he was about to give up and try another distraction, TJ cleared his throat.

"I never killed anyone before," he said. "It's harder than it looks in the movies."

Grade still had an eye on the conversation between Clay and Jones, so it took a moment for that statement to sink in. When it did, he shifted all his attention to TJ.

"What about…" He trailed off and tilted his head toward the van. "Our mutual friend who's not here anymore."

That was apparently too subtle. TJ just looked blank, his head tilted to his side like a confused, slightly skanky dog.

"Buchanan," Grade filled in for him. This time TJ screwed up his nose and shook his head slowly as he failed to follow. That left Grade with "uncomfortably direct" to get his point across. "The dead guy. In the restroom?"

Every professional habit he'd cultivated since he started this business wanted to shut him down. He ignored them in favor of his survival instinct. TJ wasn't enough. Neither was the van. If he wanted to get free and clear of the threat to end up as Ezra's sacrificial lamb, he needed the body.

Plus, the review on this job could sink him. The dark web had its own Yelp, and it was as unpleasant as you'd expect.

Grade put his finger to the side of his head and mimed pulling a trigger.

Recognition finally dawned on TJ's face as his mouth puckered around a soft "Oh." Then he laughed, a scratchy, humorless bark of a sound.

"Very funny," he said. Then his eyes narrowed as he stared at Grade. "Or wait, you  bought that? You're dumber than you look."

"I've been tested," Grade said. "I'm not. Are you saying you *didn't* kill Buchanan?"

"You aren't real quick for someone who ain't as dumb as they look," TJ muttered.

Grade bit the inside of his cheek. He didn't think of himself as a violent man, but just in that moment he could see why Clay resorted to hitting the guy right off the bat.

He crouched down and glared at TJ.

"It's been a long night, and my life—my sister's life—has been threatened, all because *someone* killed some bigshot from Lexington. So if it wasn't you…"

TJ stared at Grade for a second, and then his eyes flicked to the side to look at something over his shoulder.

Someone.

Grade twisted around to see Clay slouched against the patrol car, his head tilted back to bask in the morning sun like a lizard while Jones talked into the radio. For a moment, Grade tried to twist his brain through the mental gymnastics needed to go "You mean *Jones*?" but he couldn't quite pull it off.

"Clay."

It turned out that he couldn't even make that sound like a question.

"Yeah, Ezra's mental right-hand man," TJ said. He jerked his chin toward the Pit. "Did you see him in there? It was like he wanted me to shoot him or something. Freak."

Shit.

Grade scrubbed his hands roughly over his face and tried to think. It made sense. That didn't mean anything, though. The minute you suspected someone of something, everything about them was suddenly suspicious. Ask any cop about that.

On the other hand, if TJ was right... The last thing Clay would want would be for Grade to be off the hook.

So, shit.

Grade gave himself a second to panic and then tried to pull his brain back into line.

It didn't matter what the truth was right this minute. There was nothing he could do about it. Until he could, the best plan would be to act like nothing was wrong.

"OK," Grade said. "You don't say that in—"

He shut his mouth hard enough to make his teeth click as he heard footsteps crunch on the ground behind him. Clay put a hand on his shoulder.

"What are you two talking about?" he asked.

"Noth—"

TJ pushed himself up the van back onto his feet. He took a step forward and stuck his chin out toward Clay.

"I told him," he spat out, his face contorted with defiance. "I told him you killed Buchanan and blamed it on me. Now you gotta kill us *both*."

He said that with all the confidence of a poker player who'd just decided to raise on an idiot end hand. Grade let his head drop and pinched the bridge of his nose between finger and thumb.

"For fuck's sake," he said. "I hate this town."

# CHAPTER EIGHT

**TJ GOT TO** ride in back on the drive to town.

"Can you at least untie me?" he whined. His knee jammed into the back of Clay's seat as he shifted position. "My arms are killing me. I got rights, you know."

Clay took his eyes off the road for a second to check the rearview mirror.

The light was wrong. It was desert light—harsh white light that cast dense shadows that looked solid enough to pick up—and it looked out of place on TJ's rawboned face and two-day-old outfit.

If Clay thought about it, he could map the "right" image under that noonday glare. He reached into the side of the door for the bottle of pills instead.

"I'm going to drown you in a toilet, TJ," Clay said as he pulled the white canister out and used his thumb nail to pop the lid off. "You think I'm worried anyone is going to find out I didn't Mirandize you? Or care if they did, since I ain't a cop."

TJ scowled and squirmed in place.

"I'm just sayin'," he muttered under his breath. His lower lip was stuck out like a toddler. "No need to be a dick about it."

Clay shook his head and glanced quickly into the bottle. One pill left. He'd have to get a refill. He usually picked it up after his standing appointment with the VA therapist, but with the deal Ezra had brokered with Fisher's crew, things had been too hectic.

Still, Clay should have made time. Now, instead of picking it up from the dropout barista at the coffee shop next door to his therapist's office, he'd have to buy some from one of the over-toned moms at the spa up in the Lodge.

Could he get them closer to home? Sure, but he didn't need Ezra up his ass about it. For a career criminal, the man was risk-averse, but it wasn't like Clay was mainlining crack or bath salts.

And the pills worked. More or less. Most of the time.

Clay tossed the last one back. It was dusty and bitter, astringent as it stuck to the back of his tongue, and it scratched his throat as he swallowed. He could see Grade's disapproval out of the corner of his eye, but since Grade thought Clay was a murderer, he could stuff that.

"If that goes down the wrong way, you could get pneumonia," Grade said. He glanced up from his sister's phone, halfway through unbricking his own, and frowned at Clay. "Or worse."

"Looking for a silver lining?" Clay asked. He turned his head and opened his mouth, tongue curled up and then out, to demonstrate there was nothing left. "Sorry to disappoint."

They looked at each other for a second, and then Grade's eyes widened. "Watch the road!" He lunged over the console and grabbed the steering wheel to yank it to the side. The car veered toward the verge, hit a stone, and a big black Lexus skimmed past on the other side.

TJ made a guttural sound as he was bounced about.

"Damn," Clay said. He pushed Grade back over to his side of the car and straightened the wheel. Behind them, he saw the black car turn and stop, parked sideways in the middle of the road. On the road ahead, an identical Lexus swung in front of them and stopped abruptly. Clay kept his foot on the gas for a second as he weighed the odds, and then he snarled to himself and hit the brakes. "I guess Ezra misjudged how tight Buchanan was with his boss."

"Did you kill him?" Grade asked.

"You want to talk now?" Clay asked. He leaned over Grade and opened the glove box to get his gun out. The heavy, cool weight of it in his hand settled him. He popped the magazine in to check the load and then smacked it home with the heel of his hand. "I'd no reason to kill Buchanan, and I would have done a better job of it. TJ's just finally put three brain cells together to try and cover his ass."

In the back, TJ threw himself forward against the seat belt. It dug into his collarbone. "You're a liar! You told me to go in there, that you wanted to talk to me."

"Why? To ask you out?" Clay mocked. "You aren't my type."

"Dirty bastard," TJ said. "Buchanan was dead when I went in there. You set me up to take the fall for it. That's why I had to run."

Clay rolled his eyes. "I don't have time for this." He leaned forward to tuck the gun into the back of his jeans and then flicked the hem of his T-shirt over it. "Gotta go get shot."

Grade grabbed his arm. "Wait." He chewed on his lower lip absently as he thought. "Maybe you're both telling the truth. Who told you to go to the bathroom, TJ?"

TJ threw himself back and forth against the seat. "I told ya!" he raged. "Clay!"

"Directly?" Grade pushed. "You heard it from his own mouth, face-to-face?"

TJ stopped, his chest heaving as he panted for breath. He spat on the floor. "Of course not," he said, his voice thick with contempt and dumbass. "He was killing Buchanan."

The Lexus doors opened, and a squat man in a nice suit got out. He straightened his jacket and opened the rear passenger door. It wasn't Fisher who got out, but Clay remembered the guy from one of the meets. He was Fisher's errand boy.

So the day had not gotten any better.

Two other men got out of the car. Three from the vehicle behind.

Clay was pretty good, but this was not his preferred working environment.

"So we have a traitor," Clay said. "That explains why they're helicopter-momming Buchanan after a night out of contact. Stay in the car."

Grade smiled thinly. "That's the plan."

He hesitated for a second, his fingers tight on Clay's forearm, and then he leaned in for a hard, unexpected kiss. The tip of his tongue grazed along the seam of Clay's mouth, but he leaned back before Clay could chase that opportunity. It probably wasn't the time anyhow.

"What was that for?" Clay asked.

Grade ran his thumb along his lower lip and shrugged. "I don't know. It seemed appropriate."

"What the fuck?" TJ blurted. "Are you gay?"

There were times, Clay admitted, that he sympathized with Grade's "fucking Sweeny" sentiments. He didn't want to deal with TJ right now, but...

He cupped the back of Grade's neck and pulled him over for a much more thorough kiss. The taste of long nights and spent adrenaline was thickly familiar as Clay slipped his tongue into Grade's mouth. He caught the low whimper that tickled between their lips and then pulled away.

"You're right." Clay stroked his thumb over Grade's cheekbone and watched awareness flicker through those hazy green eyes. "That felt like the thing to do."

He winked at Grade and got out of the car and let his brain slide into neutral. It ground—briefly—on the memory of Grade's mouth and that little *noise* he made, but then the calm rolled over him.

"Hey," Clay said as he nodded at the Lexus. "Car trouble?"

Fisher's man folded his mouth into an empty smile. He took his jacket off and hung it over his arm. The shirt he had on underneath looked very white and crisp. Clay let the urge to break the beak-like bridge of the man's nose to add an accent of red to grime up all that nice cotton idle away.

"Traynor, right? Clay Traynor," the man said. "Took you long enough to join us. What was it? Last kiss for a condemned man?"

"We aren't into labels," Clay said with a smirk. He wagged his finger back and forth between them. "I didn't get your name. That's on me. I wasn't paying attention because I didn't give a shit."

The smile tightened over the man's probably perfect teeth. "I don't think you're going to be using it much," he said. "So don't worry about it. Where's Buchanan?"

Clay glanced at the heavies and then back to Fisher's mouthpiece. He shrugged.

"No idea," he said. "Where'd you leave him?"

Mouthpiece handed his jacket to one of the heavies and took a slim black phone out of his pocket. He tapped the screen and turned it so Clay could see.

"He's not answering his phone," he said. "His suitcase and his car are still at the... hotel, I guess... but the bed hasn't been slept in."

"Maybe he got lucky."

Mouthpiece licked his lower lip and put the phone away. "See," he said, "that's funny, because from what I've been told, he got the opposite of lucky."

"He's not my type," Clay said. "So his love life or lack of it—"

"Is that TJ Hall?" Mouthpiece interrupted as he pointed over Clay's shoulder.

"One of them is."

"Pretty boy or the one in the back?"

Clay hesitated for a second. His reluctance to lie and throw Grade to the wolves to buy them time caught him off guard. Lucky enough, he came up with enough flaws in that plan— Grade had no reason to play along, and TJ was too dumb to realize it would be to his advantage—that he didn't have to do it anyhow.

"What if I don't let you take him?" he said.

Mouthpiece waved a hand. "You're outnumbered," he said. "Not to mention outclassed. No offense."

"None taken."

Clay pulled his gun in one smooth motion and shot the heavy holding Mouthpiece's jacket in the foot. The bullet punched through leather and bone and jarred to a stop when it hit the concrete. Blood sprayed over the road and up the side of the car. It splattered Mouthpiece's leg, darker spots on the gray wool, as the heavy screamed and staggered backward onto his ass. He flicked his aim to the other two men, long enough to watch their eyes narrow, but didn't fire. The rest of Fisher's men cursed and pulled on him, the sound of guns being cocked loud on the quiet road.

"Well," Clay put his hands up and let the gun dangle by the trigger guard from his finger, "maybe some."

Mouthpiece leaned down and fastidiously wiped at his leg.

"That was stupid," he said. "I could kill you now and your boss couldn't even squeak about it."

"But you're not going to," Clay said. "I could have made this a lot worse."

The heavy on the far side of the car cleared his throat. "Marine?" he asked.

"SEAL."

The heavy nodded and didn't let his gun waver. "He's not lyin'," he said. "If he'd not played nice, me and Bennett would be down and he'd have a gun at your head."

Mouthpiece tightened his jaw, the muscle at the hinge clenched under his skin. "And the point of this little demonstration?" he asked. "Am I supposed to be impressed?"

"I would be," Clay said. His shoulder ached, a dull, tight pain, as he kept his hands over his head. "Me and Ezra, we're playing this straight. Whatever line someone's fed you, we don't want any trouble with Fisher."

"Want it or not," Mouthpiece said, "if anything has happened to Buchanan, you'll have it."

He gestured to one of his men, who holstered his gun and came forward warily to take Clay's off him. Once he had it, he ejected the magazine and kicked it to the side of the road, then gave the gun back.

"Who told you where to find us?" Clay asked. "Deputy Jones?"

"That's the problem with crooked cops," Mouthpiece said. "You just can't trust them."

He was right there. Clay smiled thinly as he tucked his gun away. "I'll remember that for next time."

"I wouldn't bother memorizing it," Mouthpiece said. "Not until you know if you get a next time."

He nodded toward the car. His men loped over to get TJ while Mouthpiece leaned over to retrieve his jacket from the shot man on the concrete. The man swore at him and used the side of the car to get himself back on his feet.

Clay watched coldly as they dragged TJ unceremoniously out of the back of the car by his tethered arm. Grade scrambled out too, despite what he'd been told, and grabbed at TJ's arm in protest. Clay couldn't hear what he said, but whatever it was, he backed down after one of Fisher's thugs put a practiced hand on his gun.

He backed up a couple of steps, hands held up in surrender, as they shoved TJ toward Mouthpiece's car. Clay waited until they were beside him and stepped in front of them. He pulled TJ into a rough one-armed hug.

"We'll sort this out," he promised, and then leaned in close enough that he could drop the threat directly into TJ's ear. "Keep your mouth shut, TJ."

TJ pulled away. "Or what?"

"That's enough of that," Mouthpiece said. "No talking. Mr. Traynor, you and Mr. Ezra better hope that Buchanan turns up."

"Oh," Clay said. He could feel the edge of sharp, inappropriate humor scrape at the back of his throat as he grinned, "I'm sure he will."

Bits of him, at least.

TJ was shoved—with a squawk of protest—into the trunk of the Lexus. While the rest of his men waited for him, Mouthpiece walked over. The man Clay had shot hobbled grimly at his heels; blood streaked over the road from the blown-out sole of his boot.

"Mr. Traynor," Mouthpiece said, his voice even and almost pleasant, "you have this coming."

He gave the nod and stepped to the side. That gave his henchman a clear shot at Clay's face with the brass knuckles he'd slipped on over his hand. Clay caught the hit on the side of his jaw and went down, his head full of dull red pain cut through with the buzzy high of an adrenaline hit.

Blood filled Clay's mouth, sweet and salted. He swallowed instead of spat and ran his tongue over the back of his teeth. All still present and accounted for.

"Fair enough," Clay said. His jaw hurt when he moved it, but less than he'd expected. It wasn't broken. "Only one free shot per customer, though. Next time—"

"Next time, we burn you and your boss alive in that nice house of his," the man said. He tried to put weight on his foot and grimaced as he thought better of it. It sharpened the venom in his voice. "Kids too, if they're lucky. Resale value is pretty good on—"

Clay laughed, a harsh, nasty sound, and grabbed the man's boot. He jammed his thumb into the bloody wet hole and dug down until he felt splintered bone scrape his knuckles. The man retched audibly, his face stained gray in shock, as he folded at the waist.

"You go near those kids," Clay said. His voice had slowed down, slow and thick despite the flash of quick black anger that tried to shove it out through his clenched teeth, "I'll ruin you."

Sweat stood out on the man's forehead and upper lip. He peeled his lips back from his teeth in a grimace and cocked his arm back.

"No," Mouthpiece said briskly. "That's enough."

The man made an inchoate noise of protest. "Look what he's done to me!"

"Oh, quit whining," Clay said. He let go of the man's foot. His thumb squelched like he'd had it jammed in a pie as he pulled it out, red from nail to joint.

He stuck in his thumb and pulled out a plum.

The thought skittered erratically through Clay's attention. He swallowed the crack of inappropriate laughter that pushed against the back of his tongue. "I could have done worse."

"He's right," Mouthpiece said. "Get back in the car."

For a second, it looked like the man wouldn't listen to his marching orders. Then he spat on Clay—thick and viscous against his cheek and T-shirt—and staggered back to the car. He dragged his foot behind him as he went, and no one offered him a hand.

"Don't think that means anything good for you," Mouthpiece said. He had his jacket slung over his arm, and he tucked his free hand into his pocket. With the sun on him, he looked like he should have been in *Vogue* instead of on a back road to a shithole town. "I doubt you or Ezra will make it to the end of the week. That's just not our call to make."

Clay leaned back against the road, his weight propped on one elbow. He grinned with bloody teeth and casually gave Mouthpiece the finger. For a second, they looked at each other, and then Mouthpiece shook his head and turned toward Grade.

"Think carefully about who you throw your lot in with, kid," he said. "Sinking ships go down with all hands, involved or not."

He turned on his heel and stalked back to the car. The rest of his men climbed in, doors slammed, and engines coughed to life. Both black cars pulled away and drove off down the road, back toward the Pit.

"Shit," Grade said. He came over and crouched down next to Clay, one hand gingerly laid on his shoulder. "Are you OK?"

Clay pulled the neck of his shirt up and wiped his mouth. "I've been worse."

"You sure about that?" Grade asked dryly as he grabbed Clay's arm and pulled him up off the road.

The world lurched sickeningly around Clay for a second. He closed his eyes and worked his jaw from one side to the other to make it click and his ears pop. The world had fallen back into place when he blinked his eyes open again.

"Yeah," he said, old, bad memories scratchy in the back of his throat. He walked over to the side of the road and grabbed the discarded magazine out of the grass to put back in his gun. "Pretty sure. Come on. I need to call Ezra."

The singsong refrain of the old rhyme had gotten stuck on the last line. It repeated on a loop in his head, disrupting the actionable thoughts he was trying to cobble together a plan out of.

What a good boy am I.

Not that Ezra was going to agree.

# DIRTY WORK

# CHAPTER NINE

**THE BOTTLE SMASHED** against the door to Ezra's office. Glass and whiskey sprayed out from the point of impact. It made Grade flinch, despite his best intentions, as the sharp, woodsy smell of aged liquor filled the room. Clay, sprawled in one of the uncomfortably upright wooden chairs, leg cocked up over the arm and blood still matted in his curls, didn't even tighten his shoulders.

"Fuck sake, Ez," he said. "You could have offered me a glass first. It's been a long day."

"I should offer your head to Fisher on a goddamn silver platter," he snapped. "Maybe that would be enough to save my ass."

Grade cleared his throat.

"Unless that's what whoever set this all up wants you to do," he said.

"TJ?" Ezra asked skeptically. He threw himself back down in his chair and snorted. "Pretty sure all he wants is to get out of this alive. Not that different to you, Cleaner."

Maybe. In some ways. They had certainly found themselves in the same shitty boat. The difference was that if Grade had killed Buchanan, he'd have covered his tracks better. He'd have…

OK. That would work.

Ever since he'd lost the body, Grade had run on the assumption that he was out of his depth. This wasn't his wheelhouse; he didn't solve crimes or catch murderers. He helped the bad guys get away with what they'd done.

But if he retro-engineered that process, if he played this like it was a cover-up he'd staged…

"What the hell's wrong with him?" Ezra snapped Grade out of his train of thought, his voice gravelly with annoyance. He snapped his finger and thumb loudly. "You still with us, Cleaner?"

Grade stared at him for a moment and then nodded slowly.

"I don't usually ask a lot of questions," he said. "So bear with me?"

"No," Ezra said. "You had your chance—"

Clay held up his hand. "C'mon, Ez," he said. "Maybe he's on to something. Go on, Grade."

For a second, Grade's mouth dried up and he couldn't get the words out. It felt like he was twelve again, standing at the front of the class as Mrs. Gallen encouraged him to speak up. Except this time, it was only his life on the line, not his A-plus in math. Grade squeezed a breath into his tight chest.

"How did you know Buchanan got shot?" Grade blurted out the question just as Ezra looked annoyed at him.

"I don't know," Ezra snapped. He tapped his finger hard against his temple. "The way half his brain was sprayed over the mirror. That was my first inkling. Clay?"

Clay craned his neck around to look at Grade over his shoulder. "Same," he said.

"No. Not the *method*," Grade said. "The act. How did you know he was dead? Did you hear the gunshot?"

"Yeah, sure. Of course," Ezra said. Then he grimaced and waved his hand at Clay. "I mean, I didn't, but Clay did."

Clay's eyebrows twitched together. With a last thoughtful look at Grade, he turned back to face Ezra.

"No," he said, "I didn't."

Ezra took a deep breath through his nose. "Goddamn it," he snarled as he smacked both hands down on the desk and pushed himself up out of the chair. Blood spotted the white gauze on his forearm as the muscles clenched. "You fucking told me—"

"Everyone was yelling about it," Clay said. He spread his hands and shrugged. "C'mon, Ez. I hear Buchanan's dead and I'm going to wait until I have all the facts before I give you the heads-up? Besides, he *was* dead, and TJ *did* run. At that point, you weren't asking any questions either."

For a second, Ezra looked like he was going to lunge over the table. Instead, he clenched his jaw and stepped back. He jabbed a finger in Clay's direction.

"I should have listened," he said. "Everyone always said you were a fuckup, that everything you touched turned to shit, but I'd not hear it, would I? Every time you screwed up I was there for you. I backed you up. Every time. And what the *hell* has it got me, Clay? This is my *life*. Fisher could come for my *kids*."

Clay tensed. He didn't *move*. It was just a slow, smooth clench of muscle that moved across his shoulders and down his arms. Even under the circumstances, it made Grade swallow and shift with sudden, uncomfortable awareness, but he shoved that away for later.

"I know what I owe you," Clay said. His voice was still easy, smooth despite the tight edge. "You don't have to throw it in my face. I ain't going to forget it. But don't you forget what you owe me, Ez. How many times did I take the fall to keep your rep nice and clean?"

They stared at each other.

Ezra looked down first. He rubbed his bandaged arm self-consciously. "It's my kids, Clay," he said. "They weren't meant to be part of this. This was never supposed to come home to them."

That was so breathtakingly self-serving that Grade almost said something. He didn't take jobs that involved kids—it cut into his profits, but he figured it saved on therapist bills—but there had always been plenty there to take. Maybe there'd been a time when it was enough to declare family off-limits, but Grade doubted it.

It probably wasn't the time to remind Ezra that Grade wasn't that likable, though. So he bit his tongue on that.

"So, TJ could have been telling the truth," Grade said. "Or what he *thought* was the truth. Someone told him that Clay wanted him to go into the restroom—"

"And he just went," Clay muttered. He slouched down in the chair, legs stretched out in front of him, and crossed his arms. "I need to try that the next time I wanna get laid. But all right. All right. So someone tells him to do that, and then they tell me that Buchanan is dead. Which would put them in the frame as the killer."

"Yeah," Grade said. "Or possibly, you did do it."

Clay grunted. "At this point," he said as he pinched the bridge of his nose between finger and thumb, "if I'd done it, I'd fess up just to stop having to think about it. Did TJ tell you anything after I got out of the car?"

"That he thought you might be gay—"

"Can't get anything past TJ," Ezra cracked. The joke hung uncomfortably, half friendly jibe and half awkward peace offering. After a tense moment, Clay accepted both with a wry shrug before he scooted the chair around to face Grade. "That it?"

Grade shrugged. "That I couldn't trust you."

"Just in fucking love with the obvious, that TJ," Clay said dryly. "So rather than having to track down TJ, now we have to find him and our saboteur?"

Close. But no cigar.

Grade held up two fingers. "Two saboteurs," he said. "At least. Someone told TJ to go to the restroom, someone told you he'd shot Buchanan, and someone told TJ to run because you'd pin this on him. Two could pull that off, maybe, not one."

Clay sighed and screwed his face up. He rubbed one finger along the bridge of his nose up to his eyebrows. "This whole crime thing was supposed to be simpler than Iraq," he grumbled. Ridiculous as it was, he sounded genuinely put out. "At least there I knew whose fingers to break for info."

That served as a chill reminder to Grade that he wasn't part of the deal here. His position might have improved, but he was still functionally their scapegoat. That was good. It wasn't something he should forget. Fear was a good motivator. At least, it had never let Grade down yet.

He cleared his throat. "Do you have security cameras in the bar?"

Ezra padded over to the cabinet, opened the doors, and pulled out a bottle of tequila. The worm floated in an inch of cloudy liquor at the base of the container. Ezra twisted off the cap and took a shot straight from the bottle. His face screwed up at the taste, and then he grabbed two glasses off the shelf.

"I don't exactly run the sort of business where you want a record of your dealings," he said as he sloshed tequila over his knuckles and into both tumblers. He passed one to Clay and kept the other, his fingers loosely cupped under the heavy base. The worm floated on the greasy film on top of the liquor. "Most people that drink in the Slap feel the same way."

Grade sighed. That would have made things easier. Not to mention tidier.

"That leaves the next best thing," he said. "The barman. He'll have had eyes on the bar all night. If anyone saw something, it'd be him."

There was a pause as they both thought that through. Ezra tossed back the tequila—worm and all—in one gulp. This time his nerves didn't bother to alert him as it hit his tongue.

He set the glass down and reached into his pocket for his phone.

"I can go get him," Clay said.

Ezra swiped his thumb over the screen and lifted it to his ear. The dull sound of the ringtone buzzed softly in the air.

"Your luck's gone to shit," Ezra said. "And you look like you dived down after it. I'll send someone who doesn't look like he's there to kneecap him to pick Hadley up. He has any good intel, or we hear from Fisher, I'll keep you in the loop."

There was a *lot* in how the two men glared at each other. Grade couldn't tell what any of it was, but it was there. It was *heavy*.

"Go fuck yourself," Clay said. He set his untouched tequila down on the edge of the desk and pushed it toward Ezra with one finger. "Last time you decided you were better off without me, you nearly got both of us killed. What's the address?"

Ezra pulled a sour face at the demand, but then he nodded reluctantly.

"Eighty-nine Heron Road," he told whoever was at the other end of the call. "First right after the Food Lion. Meet Clay there. He's on his way."

He hung up without any niceties and tossed the phone onto the desk.

"Don't mess this up, Clay," he said as he sank back down into his chair. It creaked as his weight settled on the leather. He was built heavier than Clay's rangy, spare build, but he wasn't fat by any means. It was all muscle. An idle part of Grade's mind calculated how long it would take to render Ezra down—in the unfortunate event it might be necessary. "We're running out of time."

Clay stood and leaned over to dip his finger, up to the knuckle, into the tequila. He stuck it in his mouth and sucked it clean.

"I can't promise that," he said. "But worse comes to worst, at least I'll have someone on hand to clean up the mess. Come on, Grade."

He turned on his heel and stalked out of the office. Grade hesitated for a second as he looked from a sour-faced Ezra to the door and back again. In the end, he went with Clay. He wasn't sure why.

OK, he was. He just hoped that under "always had bad taste in hot, dangerous dudes," there was a better reason to stick with the devil he sorta knew.

§

Heron Road was a dead-tooth street. The streets on either side had playsets out front and curtains in the window. Old men sat outside on kitchen chairs to smoke, and dogs lay sprawled in the shade in the yard. Turn onto Heron, and there were empty lots and boarded-up houses, their drives littered with cars up on bricks that had been tagged with graffiti and left to rust.

The only dog on the street was a heavyset rottweiler in a spiked collar that snarled loudly from behind a rusty chain-link fence as they drove past. No one twitched the burlap-sack curtains stapled up over the windows to see what had set him off.

"You sure Ezra gave you the right address?" Grade asked.

Clay didn't answer. His fingers just tightened around the steering wheel, and he reached down to flick the radio off. The twang and bluegrass plaint about politics, plumbing, and rednecks cut off mid-verse.

They were both quiet for a moment as they drove slowly along the road, their attention on mailboxes and the sides of houses as they searched for numbers. Most of them were gone, pried off or graffitied over. Grade lasted about three and a half houses before he cleared his throat.

"I've heard that a lot of people pay servers a living wage these days," he said. "I guess Ezra's not a fan of that idea? There's sixty-three."

Clay acknowledged that with a noise in the back of his throat. He put his foot down on the gas, and the car picked up speed.

"Pay's generous enough," Clay said. He gave Grade a sidelong look. "But staff don't get paid up-front, and Hadley only started last week. And Heron Road might not be up to your standards, but compared to where Hadley's been laying his head, it probably looks pretty palatial to him."

"Oh yeah? He from Dog Leg?" Grade asked. The old jibe at the rival town was reflex—Dog Leg was slightly better off than Sweeny, economically speaking, but who wanted to admit that— and it caught him off guard how easily it rolled off the tongue. He really *had* been back too long.

"Eddyville," Clay said flatly.

It wasn't where he said, it was the *way* he said it. Plenty of people lived in Eddyville and didn't complain about it. When someone said "Eddyville" the way Clay just had, like it was meant to mean something, and then gave a sidelong look to make sure you'd gotten the point, they meant the Castle. Kentucky State Pen.

"What? Did he get a reference from an old cellmate of yours?" Grade asked.

Clay looked amused as he pulled over to the curb in front of a shabby house with gray paint peeling off the clapboard siding. He turned off the engine and pulled the keys out of the ignition.

"There it is." Clay twisted around to face Grade, one arm cocked up over the back of the seat. "You're really invested in that, aren't you."

"In what?" Grade couldn't stop himself from asking the question, even though he was pretty sure he wasn't going to appreciate the answer.

"Being better than the rest of us," Clay said. He idly twirled his finger in the air to indicate their surroundings. "Better than Sweeny. Being the one that got out."

"You sound like my sister," Grade said. "Just because I want more than a dead-end job in a dead-end town doesn't mean I look down on the rest of you."

Clay pulled a dubious face. "Kinda sounds like you do. Yet here you are, back home with the rest of us."

"Not for long."

Clay smirked lazily. "It's already longer than you planned," he said. "Right?"

By about a year — And that wasn't something Grade wanted to talk about or think about most days.

"I don't see what my plans have to do with you," he said. "We're not friends."

Clay laughed and reached out to ruffle Grade's hair. The casual intimacy of it caught Grade off guard. Before he could decide whether to pull away from the rough caress or lean into it, Clay was finished.

"It's cute when you pretend you're not into me," he said.

"Into you?" Grade started to protest. "I am not—"

Before he could finish, Clay had gotten out of the car. The door shut on Grade's "… into you…" as Clay started down the street. His jeans were already low-slung, and the gun shoved into the waistband—black and stark against his grubby white T-shirt—made them slide lower. He looked like a walking "yeah, right" to Grade's weak lie.

"So what?" Grade muttered to himself as he unclipped the seat belt. "Just because I want to get laid doesn't mean he's right about anything else."

He scrambled out of the car and jogged along the uneven pavement until he caught up with Grade at the gate to 89 Heron Drive. It didn't look much different from the houses on either side. The Astroturf lawn was sun-faded from vivid green to a murky khaki, and there was a heavy-duty padlock on the front door, bright and shiny against the worn white-painted wood.

"I thought we were supposed to meet someone here," Grade said as Clay reached over the gate to unlock it. "Shouldn't we wait for them?"

The gate swung open halfway and jammed, crooked on old hinges. Clay stepped backward through the gap, his arms spread.

"Think of it this way," he said. "He should have been on time. And for the record? An old friend did vouch for Hadley, but he wasn't a cellmate of mine. I've never been sent to a civilian prison."

He winked—just in case Grade had missed the wriggle room he'd left himself there—and turned to head up the path. Grade followed on his heels. They had just gotten to the padlocked door—Clay's fist cocked back to hammer on the wood—when a gunshot blast echoed from inside the house.

Grade jumped and stumbled backward. It wasn't the first time he'd ever heard a gunshot. Sometimes he'd arrive at the scene and the crime hadn't finished. Or once, when they'd pre-booked and got their times wrong, it hadn't even started. That had always been distanced from him. Not his business. Literally, not until it was all over.

This time, it all felt a bit more personal.

"What the—" he spluttered.

Inside the house, a woman screamed. It had the low, raw edge that pain gave a voice, not the shrill bite of panic. For some reason, Grade reached for the door to try and get to her.

Clay grabbed his shoulder and dragged him back down the path to the fence. On the other side of the road, the rottweiler in the yard they'd passed earlier was going mad on the end of a heavy chain as it snapped its teeth at the disturbance.

"Stay—" Clay shoved him out the gate and onto the pavement. "—here. Wait for Harry."

He pulled his gun and turned back toward the house.

"Wait," Grade blurted. "Wait. I don't even know who Harry is. How am I supposed to wait for him? He could be anyone—"

Clay hesitated and then turned back. He looked exasperated.

"Harry Jenkins," he said. "You can't miss him. Big guy. Short hair—"

"No. Yeah, that's OK," Grade admittedly reluctantly. "I know Harry. My mom used to take care of his grandma."

A brief grim smile crossed Clay's face.

**DIRTY WORK**

"Small towns," he said dryly. "You gotta love 'em. Stay here."

# CHAPTER TEN

**CLAY HELD HIS** gun high and ready against his chest as he edged up to the front of the house. He made one last "stay the fuck there" gesture to Grade—who grimaced and bounced on his toes but stayed at the gate—and pressed his ear to the door. There were raised voices inside, but not close enough to the front of the house that he could make them out, and the muffled sound of heavy, ragged sobs.

The woman who'd screamed.

Knuckles in his mouth—dust and salt on his tongue as he bit down—and the sound of his own breathing loud in his ears as he slid over the rocks and sand. It hurt. It didn't hurt enough, and that scared him.

He was the only thing he could hear. The jeep was on fire, and the woman was wailing, but all Clay could hear was the static in his head.

"Give it a fucking rest," Clay muttered to his brain. "Not everything has to be about you."

He cracked his neck to one side, then the other, and breathed out slowly. The memory faded to a nervy rattle in the back of his skull and the taste of blood still in his mouth—he ran his tongue over his teeth—that might be just where he'd bitten the inside of his cheek.

"Shut up!" a man yelled. "I can't think. Shut the fuck up."

There was a thud and a yelp, and then the sobs got even more strangled and raw. Clay edged away from the door and toward the front window. The pane was blacked out by spray paint, but someone had made a half-hearted effort to scrape it off. Probably with a butter knife from the shape of the chiseled-off lines.

Clay held his breath and leaned over to peek into the house. The front room looked clear—although he was blind to the corners—and the woman was curled up in the hall. Over her shoulder, he could see into a slice of the kitchen. He didn't have eyes on the shooter, but there was blood tracked over the cracked white linoleum in the kitchen.

A decade's worth of training clicked through his mind like a shitty Filofax: option, scenario, outcome. He hesitated for a moment, his breath sticky on the back of his throat as he weighed the assessment.

But the hell with it. If he'd learned nothing else from being enlisted, he'd learned not to fuck with what wasn't broken.

Get in. Fuck them up. Deal with the fallout later.

In position. Bravo 4. Move, move, move.

Clay stepped back, shifted his weight, and kicked the door in. The heel of his boot connected in the sweet spot just under the padlock, and he felt the impact up into his knee. The lock held. It was the door that didn't. Screws ripped out of old, poorly maintained wood, and the door flew open. It slammed back into the wall and bounced back. Clay blocked it with his arm as he moved into the room and along the wall, out of line of sight from the kitchen.

Habit cleared the blind corners—nothing in them but rat shit and old sheets.

The woman on the floor screamed and tried to squirm away. She'd been shot in the shoulder, and it was a bloody mess of pulped flesh. Blood puddled on the ground under her and smeared beneath her heels as she tried to get away. He recognized her. It took him a second to realize from where.

"It wasn't my idea!" she said, her working hand raised to ward Clay off. "I didn't know it was gonna—"

…her nails dug into Clay's skin as she grabbed his arm. Her face was pale and her eyes were shiny with panic. 'Something happened. In the restroom. There's blood everywhere. It's that man who came in; the fancy one from Lexington."

"Shit," Clay swore and took off running.

It was Buchanan. He knew it. That was just their fucking luck.

"Shut the fuck up, Betsy!" a voice yelled from the kitchen. A bullet punched into the floor between Betsy's feet, and splinters flew up to dig into her ankles. She screamed and curled into a ball, her fingers buried in her dark brown hair.

Clay raised his eyebrows as he skirted around the room. "Arlo?" he said. "Is that you?"

Someone breathed heavily in the kitchen for a moment. Then, "No."

"I can smell flop sweat and BBQ bunions," Clay said. He indulged himself with a brief, exasperated look at the ceiling. His old master chief would have clipped him around the ear for letting his concentration slip, but… he wasn't here, and Clay might have to deal with being conned by Arlo. Of all the dumb bastards out there. He pulled his attention away from that thought and cocked his head to the side. "Kinda think it is you."

He took quick steps to the side, the soles of his boots scraping over the dusty floor. Just in time.

"Fuck you!" Arlo spat.

Two gunshots echoed through the small house. The bullets punched through the drywall and hissed past Clay's face. One of them hit the doorframe behind him with a solid thud, and the other smashed the blacked-out window.

Light flooded into the room. Someone yelled outside, and Clay grimaced at the thought he might have to pay the local LEOs off again. It wasn't like Ezra covered expenses. He glanced back quickly to check the street outside and got a glimpse of Grade on the other side of the car, hunkered down behind the trunk.

Not an idiot, then. Good. Only room for one of those in a bed.

"Where's Hadley, Arlo?" Clay asked.

"I'm here!" Hadley said. His voice was steady. Guthrie had said Hadley was good under pressure, unflappable. It looked like the old sergeant was still a fair judge of character, except when it came to bookies and bar fights. "Boss, is Betsy OK?"

Clay glanced at the woman on the floor. Her face was sticky with sweat and snot, and her lips were gray as more blood leaked from her shoulder.

"I wouldn't go that far," Clay said. "She's not dead."

"Stupid bitch," Arlo said, his voice ripe with contempt. It was a bit hypocritical in Clay's opinion, but people were. "She always thought she was so clever, so much better than me. TJ might have been too stupid to put the pieces together, but I'm not. I'm smarter than she thought."

Clay rolled his shoulders back to loosen them up.

"That bar's pretty low, Arlo," he drawled as he took another step to the side. He could just make out a thin slice of Arlo's rangy body in the kitchen, a greasy cowlick of hair and one prison-inked elbow. He watched as Arlo shifted his stance and raised the gun into a shooting position.

"Yeah?" Arlo sneered. "How smart do you feel now, you smug son of a—"

His muscles tightened, and Clay snapped the gun up and pulled the trigger twice. Bullets punched through the wall—not through the holes that Arlo had already shot in it, although that would have been shit-hot—and hit their target with a wet thud. Arlo staggered backward as his arm fell, suddenly noodle-limp, to his side. His legs folded under him.

*Bitch,* Clay finished the sentence for him as Arlo hit the floor. *Son of a bitch.*

Clay, gun back in a ready position, stepped over Betsy's legs. His boots squelched in the blood that had started to soak into the floor, thick and sticky.

"Holy shit," Hadley said as Clay trod more gore into the kitchen. The barman was sprawled awkwardly on the floor in the corner of, with one hand cuffed to the old white stove. "You have no idea how glad I am to see you, boss."

"Back at you," Clay said as he tucked his gun back into his jeans.

"Who the hell *is* that?" Hadley asked. "Do you know him? Is he dead?"

Clay crouched down on one knee and put two fingers under Arlo's jaw. Badly shaved stubble itched against his fingers as he pressed up into the soft wattle of flesh, but that was it. It was performative, of course. Arlo had a neat dime-sized hole right in the middle of his forehead, but apparently, Hadley hadn't caught that.

"Not yet," he lied. "Just fainted. Asshole."

He gave Arlo's cheek a light slap; it was still warm but somehow *felt* dead. Clay wondered why he'd lied. There was no reason to, and it wouldn't hold up long. Arlo was conspicuously not breathing, and his brains would start to leak soon. Sometimes, though, you just had to go with your gut, and Clay's said not to let Hadley off the hook just yet.

"What the hell did he want with you, Hadley?" Clay asked as he sat back on his heels. There was blood on the knee of his jeans, and he rubbed at it absently with his knuckles until it smudged down into another stain. "How did he even know where you live?"

Hadley got up onto his knees. He rubbed his jaw—a bruise darkening near the point of his chin—on the back of one hand.

"Ask him when he comes around," he said. "He has business with Betsy, something about her telling TJ something? I don't know. He isn't exactly the most coherent fucker."

At least one part of that story rang true.

Clay leaned back to look into the hall at Betsy. She'd passed out. Or died. It wasn't as cut and dried as Arlo's situation, but she wasn't in a good place. Either way, she wasn't about to answer any questions.

"Hey, boss," Hadley interrupted him. He cleared his throat and raised his hands, making the chain rattle against the stove. "Cut me loose here, huh? Keys were in his pocket."

"Yeah, I'm not going in there," Clay said. "You'll have to wait."

He drew his hand back and slapped Arlo again, harder this time. The crack of palm on flesh was loud in the stripped-out little kitchen. Oddly enough, Clay felt a little worse about hitting Arlo's corpse than he had about hitting Arlo. "C'mon, Arlo. Rise and shine."

Hadley snorted out a dry little bark of a laugh. "Fair enough," he said.

The front door creaked.

Shit.

Clay stood up and stepped back, the gun tucked out of view behind his leg. He caught sight of Grade over Betsy's body as the younger man edged into the house.

"I thought I told you to stay put," Clay said.

Grade pushed the door shut behind him. His gaze caught on Betsy and the puddle of blood and he paused for a second. Clay supposed he couldn't be faulted for that, but it wasn't shock on his face, just that same brief flicker of recognition. "If you took better care of yourself," Grade said. "You'd probably be sure about—behind you!"

The sound of rusted metal hinges being torn apart underlined Grade's warning, and then door of the stove caught Clay across the back. He grunted and lurched forward. His vision smeared gray at the edges—he had been hit in the head too many times—and pain twisted down his back and side in off-kilter configurations as nerves misfired and clenched muscles pulled up short. He'd felt worse. Clay caught himself on the doorframe, shook his head to clear it, and threw himself backward. He crashed into Hadley as the other man tried to push through the door. They both went down in a tangle of limbs and cursing, the stove door jammed awkwardly between them.

It wasn't a pretty fight.

Of course, off the mat, they never were. People thought fights were like they saw in the movies, all roundhouse kicks and technique. In real life, all that went to shit the first time some bastard jammed a dirty thumb in your eye and a knee to your kidney. It was messy and bloody and involved a lot of grunting.

The two of them scuffled on the grimy linoleum, blood smeared out around them. Clay managed to pin the stove door—and Hadley's cuffed arm—to the floor with one knee while gripping handful of Hadley's hair. He smacked the other man's head off the floor a couple of times, before his grip slipped and he was just left with a handful of dirty blond strands in his fingers.

From the corner of his eye, he saw Grade skirt around the edge of the fight, between the smears of gore. Good plan. Get out while you can. Clay couldn't hold it against him.

Hadley drove a knuckly punch up into Clay's armpit, the pain scorching precisely through his arm and down his ribs—and managed to wrestle them both over so he was on top. He jammed the edge of the stove door into Clay's throat and held it there while he scrabbled for the gun in Clay's waistband.

Clay slapped his hand away twice as he choked. He grabbed Hadley's face and hooked his thumb into the man's mouth. A yank pulled Hadley's cheek out grotesquely, his lip splitting at the corner and his eyes wet as the pain bit. He recoiled, drool and blood slick on his chin, and the pressure on Clay's throat let up. Before he could take advantage, Hadley grabbed the door in both hands and brought it down like a hammer. Clay got his arms up enough to block—his braced forearms at first hot with pain and then heavy and numb—as Hadley hammered at him.

After a handful of blows, Hadley flung the door to the side—still tethered to his wrist—and went for Clay's gun again. This time Clay couldn't get his arms to cooperate enough to block. Hadley lurched back as he scrambled awkwardly to his feet, stove door dangling from one hand and gun in the other. He stepped back and spat a bloody gob of spit to the side.

"No hard feelings," Hadley said. The gun twitched from Clay's center of mass up to his face. It didn't waver. "Some opportunities are just too good to pass up. So I'm afraid I'll have to end our association."

Clay grinned up at him. He could feel the blood slick and wet on his teeth.

"Get on with it," he said. "I ain't got all day."

Hadley shook his head. "People said you had a death wish, but—"

"I think he meant me," Grade said.

Clay hadn't, but he wasn't going to argue. He tilted his head back and squinted up at Grade as the younger man straightened up and aimed Arlo's gun at Hadley.

"Put it down, kid," Hadley said. "You're going to hurt yourself."

Grade tightened his grip on the butt of the gun and shifted his stance. "Do you know how many people were shot by toddlers last year?" he asked. "Over two hundred. I have a feeling it's not that hard. Get away from him."

For a second, Hadley's finger flexed around the trigger of the gun, skin pulled tight over his knuckles. Still sprawled out on the floor, Clay bit his lower lip as the almost sexual anticipation tightened his muscles.

"Big talk," Hadley said. "Do you think you have the balls to kill someone, to put a bullet in their head and watch them die?"

Clay propped himself up on his elbow and wiped the back of his hand over his mouth. "You know better than that," he said.

"Stay the fuck down," Hadley warned him coldly.

Clay sat up instead. The gun's muzzle was close enough he could smell the gun oil.

"It's like whiskey," he said. "Everyone thinks they can hold their liquor the first time they belly up to the bar. It's only the morning after that regrets set in."

Hadley glared at him, but his finger didn't move on the trigger. He worked his jaw from one side to the other as he flicked his attention from Clay to Grade and then back again. Blood trickled from his nose, and he absently licked it away as it puddled on his top lip.

"Yeah," he said. "Lot of things work that way. By the time you have second thoughts, it's too late to climb back out. Is that what you want for him, Clay? To be like us?"

*No.* The realization was a sharp-edged, unexplainable object lodged in Clay's throat. He swallowed, but the scratchy knowledge that he *didn't want that* wouldn't budge. He clenched his jaw on admitting it.

Grade cleared his throat. "For the record," he said, starch in his voice. "If you don't get away from him, we're all going to find out if I have the balls to pull the trigger."

Temper grimaced Hadley's lips back from his teeth. For a second, it looked like he was going to call Grade's bluff. Then he backed away slowly, careful of his footsteps on the bloody floor, toward the back door. The gun stayed aimed squarely at Clay's face.

"We're not done with you," Clay said as he got his feet under him. "You're not going anywhere."

Hadley grinned, the wide, personable smile that said, "Trust me, the whiskey is worth the price."

"You can tell Pulaski there to shoot me," he said as he reached behind him to fumble for the handle of the door. "But he better have damn good aim, because I do. If he doesn't put me down with a kill shot, I'll blow your brains all over his feet."

Grade took a breath. Hopefully, the muttered "Ugh" at that idea was low enough that only Clay heard it.

"Did you kill Buchanan?" he asked.

The corners of Hadley's eyes crinkled. Apparently, that was a funny question for some reason.

"That's a bit complicated," he said.

Grade took a step forward. "But you did drive me off the road. You stole the remains from my van." He tilted his head toward the two bodies on the floor. "You and these two were in it together? I *knew* I'd recognized her at the bar."

The latch finally clicked free, and Hadley pushed the door open behind him. He stepped backward, down onto the step that led to the backyard.

"Arlo wasn't exactly part of the plan. Well, neither were you," he said. "But I saw a way to use you to my advantage, so I did."

His foot came down on something that made him stagger. He looked back and down to see what it was as he recovered his balance. The momentary lapse in attention was an opportunity, and Clay scrambled to his feet. For the first time since they'd met, Grade didn't seem inclined to analyze, argue, or question why something did—or didn't— need to happen. In fact, he almost shoved the gun into Clay's hand. The familiar weight of a weapon felt almost reassuring.

Clay swung around and raised the gun in one smooth movement. He pulled the trigger just as Hadley turned back to them.

The gun jammed. Arlo, that stupid son of a bitch.

Hadley had flinched in expectation of getting shot. Once he realized that he wasn't going to be, he laughed with no real humor in the noise.

"You tried," he said. "Can't fault you for that."

Clay threw the gun at him. It didn't have much impact, but confusion made Hadley falter for a second. Long enough for Clay to throw himself at Grade, taking them both down into a slide that ended behind the overturned kitchen table. It wasn't much of a shelter, but…

Gunfire echoed around the kitchen as bullets punched through the table and gouged holes in the floor. A few strays went through the thin plasterboard walls, and Clay hoped the street was as dead as it looked.

The noise finally faded away.

Clay scrambled inelegantly out from behind the table.

"Stay," he barked at Grade as he ran after Hadley.

"Not a dog!" Grade yelled from behind him.

The lot at the back of the house was all hard-packed dirt and dead plants in the flower beds. The chain-link fence, layered with fake plastic vines to give some privacy, was still rattling. Clay followed. He scrambled up the fence and dropped down the other side into a neat green garden with a well-used children's playset kicked over on its side.

A big, round yellow lab lay on the deck at the back of the house. It lifted its head to watch as Clay ran across the garden and down the side of the house. There was a gate through to the front, but someone had already kicked it open.

Clay burst through it at a dead run and down the drive to the road. He skidded to a stop at the dropped curb as he spun in a circle to look up and down the street. His eyes flicked over the old blue pickup on the other side of the road on the first scan, but then swung back. He'd only seen it once: when Hadley had rolled into town with a backpack and a sob story. There was a faded "Getting outdoors in Eddyville" decal on the bumper. Clay had thought it was funny since, you know, outdoors had been the last thing Hadley had been getting.

The engine had sounded like it was on its last legs when it turned over.

It still did.

"Son of a bitch."

Clay bolted across the road. He slammed into the side of the pickup as it pulled out and grabbed the door handle. It was locked. Clay smacked his fist against the window, and Hadley looked at him briefly, then put his foot down on the gas.

For a few feet, Clay hung on to the door as he ran alongside the pickup. Then he gave up with a frustrated snarl and let go. He fell behind as the truck sped down the road and screeched around the corner. For a minute, he stood there in the middle of the road, his jaw clenched so hard the bones hurt. Then someone laid on their horn behind him.

He turned around. A battered purple-grape Toyota was stopped behind him, with an annoyed woman glaring at him over the wheel. She leaned on the horn again.

Clay gave her the finger and got out of the way.

He stood on the side of the road and patted himself down. He still had his phone on him, shoved in his back pocket, but his cigarettes were back in the car.

Fuck it. He rolled his head from one side to the other and listened to his neck crackle. Then he started down the street to take the long way back to his car. Ezra could wait on the bad news. Clay hadn't gotten to kill anyone, and he needed to indulge at least one bad habit today before anyone else tested him.

"Huh." Harry took a can of soda out of Hadley's fridge and tossed it to Clay with a smirk. "It'd probably have gone differently if you'd had backup, huh?"

Clay caught the soda in one hand. The metal wasn't chilled. It didn't look like Hadley had bothered to hook up most of the appliances. He turned it around to check the brand. Crush orange soda.

"Is there a beer in there?" he asked.

Harry glanced in and then closed the door. "Nope."

"Don't fucking lie to me," Clay said.

Harry ignored him. He jerked his thumb at the stain in the hall. "What about the woman?" he asked.

"I patched her up," Clay said. "Enough to get her to the Community Hospital over in Doglan—"

"Dog Leg," Harry corrected him absently. He shrugged at Clay's glare. "No one is gonna know who you mean if you call it Doglan."

Clay wiped bloody hands on his jeans. It had been a while since he'd had to patch so many people up. These days, his job usually required the opposite. He popped the tab on the soda and took a drink. It was disgusting. It was probably sugary enough when it was cold, but warm it tasted like a melted cough drop.

"She lost a lot of blood, but she's got a good chance to pull through. The arm might not, but it's not like I shot her. I sent Abbot with her. He'll hang around until she wakes up and make sure she doesn't run her mouth."

He took another swig of the soda—it wasn't an acquired taste, still gross—and leaned back against the scarred counter. They both looked at Arlo, sprawled out on the floor. He was still wearing the charred sneakers that Clay had shoved in the oven last night. Clay hadn't noticed that earlier.

"He did," he said.

"Didn't think Arlo had it in him." Harry scratched the side of his jaw and scowled. "I didn't think Hadley did either. I thought he'd come with a reference?"

"Yeah. He did. Two months ago, Hadley got out of the state pen, and Guthrie asked us to give him a chance. He'd played hero over some girl and got six years for manslaughter when some kid turned out to have a glass jaw—served three. I checked. That's the weird thing. So how the fuck did he pull this off?"

Harry shrugged and held out his hand for the soda. Clay handed it over.

"I don't know," Harry said. He took a drink and pulled a face before he tossed the can in the sink. "Jesus, that's disgusting. Maybe he just saw an opportunity and seized the day? Fuck, after three years in prison, I'd want more than another forty doing nine to five in this shithole."

Maybe. It was a pretty complicated plan to come up with on the fly, though. And Hadley hadn't held that gun like it was his first time.

That was Ezra's problem, though. Clay was the muscle, not the brain. He liked the work/life balance that gave him. He ran his fingers through his hair and picked out splinters of plywood from the tangles.

"I should introduce you to Grade," he said. "The two of you have a lot in common."

"Yeah, I'm still hoping to patch things up properly with Lanie," Harry said, "so I gotta pass. Besides, small town. His ma was probably my granny's hairdresser or something. Where is Pulaski anyhow?"

Clay gave Arlo's outstretched arm a nudge with the toe of his boot. "Looking in the shed for something to wrap the body in."

"Useful."

"Yeah."

Clay's phone went off in his pocket. It was Ezra's ringtone, the chorus to "Copperhead Road." They listened to it for a while, and then Clay pulled it out and turned it off.

"He's pissed," Harry said.

"Fuck me. Really?"

Clay pulled a pack of cigarettes out of his pocket. He'd just lit one, over Harry's pointed throat clearing, when Grade pushed the back door open with his foot. There was a roll of tarp over his shoulder, he stank of bleach, and he looked pleased with himself.

"I found Buchanan," Grade said cheerfully. He turned his head to point with his chin toward the garden. "He's in the shed."

Clay inhaled a lungful of smooth, warm smoke and then pinched the end of the cigarette out. He flicked the butt onto Arlo's body, where it singed a hole in the middle of a cartoon pole dancer's stomach.

"At this point," he admitted, "I am *not* sure if that counts as good news or not."

Harry grunted. "Pretty sure he's going to end up in my truck," he grumbled. "So not great news for me."

Fair point.

# CHAPTER ELEVEN

**GRADE WEDGED THE** end of a flat-head screwdriver under the dented lid of the drum and then put his weight on the handle. It resisted for a second and then popped free with a hollow clunk. He lifted it, tapped it against the lip of the drum so it wouldn't drip everywhere, and then set it against the wall.

None of the other three men in the room moved for a second. Finally, Ezra made an aggrieved sound in the back of his throat and stepped forward. He screwed his face up in distaste as he leaned over to look in at the… remains.

"Ah, Jesus," he said. "It's like Hell's gumbo."

Grade tapped the side of the drum with his foot. There wasn't a lot of room in there, but it was enough for the bits to wobble about as the liquid sloshed.

"That's Buchanan," he said, "so I'm off the hook."

Ezra pointed at him. "That's fucking disgusting is what that is," he said. "And the contract was you get it *out* of my bar."

"And then you told me to bring it back," Grade said. He bit the inside of his cheek on a tart "Make up your mind." It was rarely a good idea to push your luck.

"Yeah," Ezra agreed. He stepped back and leaned against his desk. His shirtsleeves were rolled up to his elbows, and he scratched absently around the edges of his dressing. "Bring it back… *before* Fisher's men got wind that something had happened to his bagman. Unfortunately, they were more on the ball than you."

Grade frowned at him and opened his mouth to argue. "You said—"

"Fisher's men already saw you," Clay interrupted him. He pointed with his chin at the drum. "And they probably aren't going to be happy about *that*…"

"Fuck knows, I'm not," Ezra grumbled under his breath. "I was going to make stew for the kids."

Clay ignored the interruption. "So you're still on the hook, same as the rest of us," he said. "Get used to it. And put the lid back on before someone knocks the bastard over."

The answer wasn't what Grade had wanted. He couldn't pretend to be surprised either, though. "Get out of jail free" cards only worked in Monopoly. He picked up the lid and slapped it back on.

"Wait," Clay said. He looked at Grade. "You sure that's Buchanan? We're not going to decant him for Fisher and it turns out to be whoever lived in that house before Hadley rocked up?"

Grade paused as he rested the screwdriver on the top of the drum. "You want to take another look?"

"No," Ezra said. "Besides, Clay never met Buchanan. I did. That was him."

"You met him once," Clay pointed out. "Grade spent two hours getting intimate—"

Grade grimaced. "Not the way I'd describe it."

"Up close and personal?"

"Not better," Grade told him. "But I get your point. This is the guy I cut up. I recognize my work."

Ezra looked at Clay. "Satisfied?"

Clay scratched behind his ear and pulled a dour face. "In a lot of ways, no," he said. "Get the lid back on and get it out of my office."

Apparently, Grade might still be on the hook, but he wasn't part of the crew. The three men leaned their heads together in grim conversation, while Grade was left on the outside to get on with his job. It was how he liked it. The rule of thumb was usually knowing anything meant you knew too much, but… this was hardly usual.

Grade used the butt of the screwdriver to hammer the lid into place. He picked up bits and pieces of the conversation as he worked.

"… still don't know what happened," Ezra said. "If we come up with one story and TJ contradicts us—"

"Deal with that when it happens," Clay interrupted him. "Look, we know Hadley was involved. The woman—Betsy—she was the one who told me Buchanan had been shot. Hadley had to be the one who set TJ up. We aren't getting out of this scot-free—"

"No, because we look like morons," Ezra said.

Out of the corner of his eye, Grade saw Harry lean in and press his finger against the desk to make a point.

"We have her. She can fill in the blanks. Whoever the she is—"

Grade braced his foot against the base of the drum and levered it up onto its rim. He balanced it there as he cleared his throat.

"I didn't recognize her at first either," he said. "Not until I saw her and Arlo together. That was Elizabeth, Arlo's cousin."

"Fuck off," Ezra said in surprise. "Elizabeth Hall? She used to work at the Choke."

Grade shrugged. "Yeah, a couple of years ago," he said. "She was friends with my sister. They went to Lexington together a couple of times. I saw all the photos on Twitter. She had stripper heels tattooed on one shoulder and sneakers on the other."

He looked at Clay, who pulled a dubious face.

"She had *something* tattooed on her shoulder," he said. "There wasn't much left of it. It could have been a shoe."

"She took off a couple of years ago," Grade said. "Dory thought she'd hooked up with some big shot in Lexington who had come through for her."

"I guess that didn't last, then," Ezra said. He closed his eyes and scratched the back of his neck. "Fine. I'll call Fisher and try to sell this story to them. The rest of you get out of here. If the shit's going to hit the fan, it won't be until later tonight. That's when the fish come up to feed."

Clay hung back while Harry held the door so Grade could manhandle the drum out into the hall. It scraped against the concrete floor as they shoved it down into a storeroom. Harry clapped a hand on Grade's shoulder on the way out.

"Don't worry about it," he said. "Ezra could sell a strip club membership to a nun. He'll get Fisher's crew off our back. Do you need a lift?"

"No," Grade said. "I got one."

§

It took another hour before Clay came out of the Slap. He looked tired and irritated, the sort of dull, exasperated anger that you felt for something you couldn't do anything about, and was halfway through lighting a cigarette. He stopped when he saw Grade perched on the hood of his car, his feet braced against the bumper and weight leaned back against his arms.

"Hey," Grade said.

Clay rubbed his thumb along his jaw. He'd washed his hands, but there was still blood in the creases of his knuckles and around his nails. The corner of his mouth curled in a lazy nod to charm.

"You need something?" he asked.

Grade slid off the car and brushed dust from the backside of his trousers.

"Do you?" he asked.

Clay snorted as he finished lighting up. He took a drag and exhaled a plume of gray smoke down his nose.

"That's a bit of a long list today," he said. "You want to be more specific?"

Grade ran his fingers through his hair. The ghost of yesterday's hair gel was sticky in patches as he flattened the light brown quiff down.

"I don't want to go back to the house and pretend it might not be the last time I see my family," Grade said. "Meanwhile, you're hot and have been on the raw edge of needing *something* for hours, so…"

He trailed off with a shrug.

Clay flicked ash onto the ground and raised his eyebrows. "So… why not?" he finished Grade's sentence for him. "Wow. I'm going to blush."

Grade rolled his eyes. He walked over and hooked his fingers into the waistband of Clay's jeans, worn denim soft against his fingertips and lean muscle taut against his knuckles. Something imperceptible tensed in Clay, and Grade felt the old, scratchy fear in his throat that he'd read it wrong. It happened.

He kissed Clay anyhow. The taste of smoke and whiskey caught on Grade's tongue as he deepened the kiss, the sudden demand of *hunger* in the pit of his chest unexpected. He had to make himself pull away and step back.

"So why not," he repeated. The warmth of Clay's body distracted him. He had to make himself step back again to stop from touching. Grade took a deep breath that *didn't* smell of Clay and tried to look like he wasn't the one who wanted this more. "Do you have anything better to do?"

Clay dropped the cigarette to the ground and scuffed it out to smoke and bits of charred paper with the toe of his boot.

"Yeah, I do," he said. Then he reached out and grazed his thumb over Grade's kiss-damp lower lip. "But what the hell. What's the point in being a criminal if you can't do what you want, right?"

§

The white towel slung low over Clay's lean hips as he padded out of the bathroom. Drops of water ran down his stomach and beaded in the hair on his thighs. The scratchy black-and-red tattoos that covered his arms spread over his shoulders and along his collarbones before they petered out. His torso was decorated with scars instead, a spray of shiny, knotted skin that ran down one side of his body from his nipple to the sharp jut of hip bone above the towel.

Clay tucked wet curls back behind his ears. The streaks of blond in the brown were more obvious when it was soaked. He spread his arms to pull his skin tight over the play of hard muscle and make the scar tissue slide and tighten.

"Gonna ask?"

Grade leaned back on the bed, arms braced behind him, and shook his head.

"No."

Clay raised his eyebrows, arms still outstretched. Grade wasn't going to complain. The play of taut muscle was nice to watch. "You're not curious?"

He didn't need to be. It had been a car accident. Grade could see the diagonal void where the seat belt had protected his skin when what he'd been wearing had burned. The telltale char pattern—skin, in Clay's case—down his left side was distinctive and easy enough to replicate on a corpse if you remembered to factor in movement.

That was what they liked to call—in the business—a mood killer. People might think it was hot when Sherlock Holmes read people, but when your specialist subject was the stigmata of violent death… suddenly it was creepy. It had been in the past, anyhow.

"It's not a date," Grade dodged the truth with another truth. "I'm not here to get to know you."

Clay lowered his hands to the towel and toyed with the loose knot that held it in place. He wriggled his eyebrows at Grade.

"You don't even want to see how far they go down?" he asked.

Grade ran his eyes down Clay's body, from the crosshatched skull on his shoulder to the last lick of raised pink scar tissue that cupped his hip bone. He skipped his eyes over the damp drape of the towel to the taut muscles of Clay's tanned thighs. His skin felt too small for his bones and uncomfortably hot as he tried not to squirm. Lust settled heavily in his balls and pulled them up tight to his body.

"I can see where it ends," he pointed out. "The towel kind of killed the element of surprise."

Clay smirked, turned around, and dropped the towel. The scars were a lot less severe on his back, but they wrapped around his ribs and dribbled down his side to scour dimples into the lean curve of his ass.

"Shows what you fucking know," he said over his shoulder. "I always got something in my back pocket…. which was the problem."

Grade wasn't going to ask on principle now. He pushed himself up into a sitting position and leaned forward, his elbows propped on his knees and hands dangled between them.

"You know what I do," he said. "You've seen it. Did you need to stage the whole shower thing to make sure I wouldn't freak out over a few scars?"

Clay turned back around and slid his hand down to lazily wrap his tattooed fingers around his semi-erect cock. The thin skin creased as he dragged his hand back along it. His lazy smirk didn't slip, but his dark eyes went hard under the straight lines of his eyebrows.

"I don't know what you're talking about," he said. His voice dragged, thick and slow with something dangerous, as he folded his lower lip between his teeth. "You gotta get clean if you want to get dirty, and that's what you're here for, right? Now, you want to get some of my grime on you, City Boy?"

Heat flushed through Grade in a painful, ragged rush. It left his ears sunburn hot and his mouth dry. His cock was suddenly, uncomfortably hard, pressed against the zipper of his pants insistently enough he thought he could count the metal teeth.

The sudden gut-punch of lust wasn't what Grade had expected. He'd come here to get fucked, sure, but that was just… mechanical. Grade had gotten wound too tight, and he needed to take some of the tension off his internal springs before they snapped. Just to stop the roundabout of all the various ways he'd screwed up.

This wasn't that. It was a ten on a dial meant to be turned to seven, and Grade was bizarrely resentful about that. There wasn't enough blood in his brain right now to explain why exactly, but it felt like he'd missed a step somehow.

Clay wasn't supposed to know him well enough to press the buttons needed to leave Grade hot and hurting. It didn't feel like Grade was in control anymore, and his body might like that, but *he* didn't.

"I... I'm just here to get off," he said. His voice was dry, and every time his eyes strayed down to Clay's thick, slick cock, the words caught in his throat. "Let's not make it complicated."

Clay laughed at him.

"Fucking's always complicated," he said. "If anyone tells you any different, they're lying."

Grade's shoulders tightened, as if he'd just been caught out on something. Except he hadn't. Not yet.

"It's just sex."

"It's people," Clay said. "People make everything complicated. Except me. I'm an open book. With its cock out, in case you wanted to join in before I finish the job myself."

Grade swallowed hard. This had been his idea. He wanted this—needed it, still—so he didn't know where the sudden conviction he should take the out Clay offered came from. He supposed it didn't matter; he wasn't going to do it. His brain had just earned the right to say "I told you so" later.

"Most of my hookups don't involve this much talking." He stood up and pulled his T-shirt off over his head. "It threw me off."

He dropped the T-shirt onto the floor and walked over to pull Clay into a kiss. For a moment he was doing all the work, and then Clay's hand slid around his hip and pulled him closer.

His cock pressed against Grade's hip, and his tongue shoved roughly into Grade's mouth as he took over the kiss. It was rough and impatient, all sharp teeth and short, ragged gasps of air. Stubble scraped at his lips, and Grade tasted Imperial Leather with an undertaste of smoke.

Clay broke it. He stepped back and smirked at the involuntary groan that escaped Grade.

"Yeah," he said. "If I were you, I'd get over that. You should know by now, I like to talk."

He braced his hand against Grade's chest and pushed him toward the bed. Grade resisted for a second but then went along with it. His knees hit the edge of the mattress, and he fell back onto it. Clay crawled on top of him, all heavy muscle and skin that was still damp from the shower. He straddled Grade's hips, cock flushed dark and tilted up toward his stomach. It twitched with his heartbeat, the long vein on the underside proud.

Grade ran his hands up Clay's thighs, over the clenched bands of muscle and damp skin. His thumbs grazed over the trailing edges of scar tissue as he headed toward—

"Ah," Clay said as he caught Grade's hands and wrapped long, inked fingers around his wrists. He pushed them back down onto the bed, his body slanted over Grade and close enough that his cock was trapped between their bodies, hard as it pressed against Grade's stomach. "That's not how we're playing this."

The muscles in Grade's shoulders tightened as he tried to break Clay's grip. It didn't work. Clay just tightened his hold enough to make Grade bite the inside of his cheek in discomfort, and pinned Grade's wrists to the mattress. After a second of struggle, Grade gave up and relaxed under Clay's weight. His heart stuttered against his rib cage with a mixture of arousal and anxiety.

"Didn't know there were rules," he said.

Clay grinned again, loose and wicked. He dropped a quick, rough kiss on the corner of Grade's mouth.

"You like rules," he said, between Grade's lips. "Bet you never got in trouble at school."

Grade felt the heat scorch over his cheekbones. He shifted position against the mattress, sheets rucked up under his hips and elbows. It was stupid to be defensive about a squeaky-clean rep from a decade ago, but…

"I knew those rules."

Clay smiled and bit the edge of Grade's jaw. "And I know these," he said. "That's what makes it fun."

He rolled off Grade and threw himself back dramatically. The dark sheets made his skin look brighter—honey gold splashed with ink. He tucked one arm behind his head, tense muscles defined as they bunched under his skin, and ran his free hand down his chest in a slow caress as he waited for Grade to prop himself up on his elbow.

"You wanted to play jungle gym with my cock," Clay reminded Grade as he idly flicked the tight light-brown nub of his nipple with his thumb. He paused long enough to wave his hand at the long, taut sprawl of his body. "Feel free. But you get to do all the work."

Clay reached out without bothering to look and grabbed a bottle left on the bedside table. He tossed it to Grade. The plastic was sticky and smelled of…

"Is that… cake?" Grade asked, lust stalled briefly as he sniffed his fingers.

Clay grinned. "Black forest gelato," he said. "What? I don't deserve nice shit?"

Grade paused, head tilted, and stared at Clay. "Was that on purpose?"

"No," Clay admitted after a second. "But it will be next time I use it. Now, you gonna get on or what?"

He waited, eyebrows raised, and Grade rolled his eyes as he got up onto his knees. It wasn't that Clay being an asshole was a problem—it was a feature. If they survived the next twenty-four hours, the last thing Grade wanted was anything to tie him down to this shithole town. But it being foreplay was unexpected. Grade popped the cap on the bottle and squeezed a blob of clear, ferociously chocolate-cherry scented lube onto his fingers.

"And what if I wanted to fuck you?" Grade asked as he knee-walked up the bed until he could sit back onto Clay's thighs. He cupped Clay's balls in his wet fingers and then glazed the hard length of his cock in the lube. The muscles in Clay's stomach hitched at the contact, suddenly rock-hard under tanned skin and scars, but his expression didn't change. "What are you going to do then?"

"Turn over?" Clay said. His voice stayed even, but his breath hitched briefly in the back of his throat as Grade pressed the pad of his thumb against the base of Clay's cock. There was a flicker of lazy challenge in his eyes as he asked, "Want me to?"

The thought made Grade's balls tighten, a tug of interest that ran back along his taint to his asshole. Grade could imagine Clay sprawled out under him, those tattooed shoulders slick with sweat and his ass *tight* around Grade's cock. It might even shut Clay up for a second.

Probably not, though, and...

"No," Grade said. "I don't."

Clay's grin widened. "Didn't think you would."

"Not this time," Grade said.

His brain stuttered over that briefly. This was meant to be a one-off. It was a faux pas to bring up repeat performances. That was a rookie mistake. Luckily Clay seemed to have missed Grade's fumble. He just waited expectantly.

Grade rolled back off his knees into a squat and stood up. The mattress shifted under his weight as he unbuttoned his trousers and pushed them down over his thighs. His cock nudged against his stomach, precum sticky on his skin, as he bent down.

Clay just lay there to enjoy the view for a bit and pushed himself up into a sitting position to help Grade strip. He licked wet kisses over Grade's thighs as he dragged the crumpled chinos down to Grade's ankles so he could step out of them. The muscles in Grade's thighs quivered in response as little jolts of sensation fired under his skin and shot straight to his crotch.

Clay ran his hands up the back of Grade's thighs in a slow caress, his palms rough with calluses. He tucked one leg under him and worked his way up until he bit a kiss into the tender skin at the crease of Grade's thigh. It made Grade's legs tremble as the sting of pleasure-pain made his cock so hard it ached. He reached down and worked his fingers into Clay's messy curls, wet and cold against his palm.

"I thought I was doing all the work," he said.

Clay laughed, his breath warm against wet, bruised skin, and turned his head to mouth at Grade's balls. He sucked on the fine skin, hard enough to make Grade whimper with sensation—it didn't matter if it felt good or bad. In the moment, it just *felt*.

"Just making sure you were all loosened up."

This time he let Grade feel his teeth as he sucked on his balls, the edges just *there* against tender flesh. Then he dropped back down onto his elbows and let his gaze travel slowly up Grade's body, with an appreciative pause at his cock before he made it up to his face.

"Doesn't seem to have worked," he said.

Grade snorted at him and got back down onto the bed one knee at a time. He grabbed the bottle to get more lube and then stretched forward to set it back down on the table. Clay shifted his weight onto one elbow so he could stroke his hand up the exposed length of Grade's side. His fingers tested the muscle in Grade's waist before they bumped over the bony slats of his ribs.

"Not much meat on your bones," he said. "Both of us are going to have bruises tomorrow."

Reaction to the dark promise in Clay's voice shivered down Grade's back. He tried to ignore it—or at least not let it show it on his face—as he straightened up. Lube puddled stickily in his palm and coated his fingers. Some of it dripped off onto Clay's skin as Grade reached back and slid coated fingers into his own ass. It was an easy, familiar pleasure that worked up into his stomach and then down to settle in his balls.

"You bite your tongue when you do that," Clay said. He stuck his own tongue out to demonstrate, the end of it pinched between his teeth. The curl of it managed somehow to be lewd. Then Clay released it and licked his lower lip slowly as he looked up at Grade with hooded dark eyes. "I want to see if you do it when you come."

Grade swallowed and tried to pinpoint exactly *how* he'd lost control of this. His cock didn't care, but he'd like to know for future reference. He couldn't pinpoint it at the moment, but he pushed it to the back of his mind for later.

He shifted back and reached down to wrap his hand around the base of Clay's cock. Blood pulsed against his fingers, quick and hard, as he adjusted the angle. Under him, Clay made a low, raw sound in his throat as he reached up to grab the bars of the headboard. The tendons in his wrist stood out as he tightened his grip, muscles clenched under his skin, and pulled the scars tight.

Grade consciously tried not to bite his tongue as he pushed down on Clay's cock. The blunt pressure against his ass made his stomach clench and his breath catch. It ached as he spread around the thick shaft, a dull pressure between his hip bones, but the aftertaste of sticky, hot pleasure followed like a chaser. It clenched in his stomach and settled, heavy and solid, in his balls.

Grade closed his eyes as he focused on the physical, the itch of pleasure-parched nerves under his skin, eager for the *more* that knotted in his stomach and caught in his throat. The thickness of Clay's cock in his ass, the slippery warmth and texture of bare skin as he pulled himself up and then thrust back down. His lips tasted like salt when he licked them, and his cock rubbed along Clay's stomach as he rocked his hips forward.

"What sort of name is Grade anyhow?" Clay asked. His accent had thickened and slowed, molasses dragged off his tongue. The question interrupted Grade's focus on his body and pinned him back down into the now. He opened his eyes and stared down at Clay, whose body was a long, taut line tethered to the headboard with a white-knuckled grip. "Who calls their kid Grade Pulaski? Your dad didn't like you even before he fucked off?"

It took a second for Grade to shuffle together enough neurons that weren't preoccupied with fired nerve-endings and the dull throb of pleasure that ran from his ass to his balls on a hot wire strung through his taint. He licked his lips.

"Now?"

Clay grinned and thrust up roughly. His cock slid deeper into Grade and ground against his prostate, a complicated burst of pleasure that made Grade bite down on the inside of his cheek. He gasped for breath as he reached back to brace one hand on Clay's thigh.

"Been thinking about it," Clay said.

"It's a nickname," Grade said.

Clay reached down between their bodies and grabbed Grade's cock. He stroked it roughly, and Grade groaned as he tightened his fingers on Clay's leg.

"For?"

"I skipped a grade in school," Grade said in frustration. His body felt strung on a very taut wire that hooked into his balls, and he wasn't in the mood to talk about the assholes he'd grown up with. Or that it had been two grades. Or that all these years on, he still called himself by the same nickname. If he'd wanted to get into all that, he'd have found a therapist to fuck. It didn't help that Clay still had a hold of his cock, callused thumb nudged up under the slick head as Grade tried not to squirm.

"Why—oh, god—ask now?"

Clay pursed his lips and shrugged. "You weren't paying attention," he said. "Now you are. If you want to fuck me, Skipped-a-Grade Pulaski, you fuck me, not whatever lives rent-free in your head. And, you know, I did tell you I liked to talk."

Grade leaned down and kissed Clay. It seemed like the only way to shut him up. He felt Clay's surprise on his indrawn breath, and the body under his relaxed as Clay kissed him back. Long fingers cupped the back of his neck as Clay leaned up into the press of lips and tongue.

Some little voice in the back of Grade's head said he'd made a mistake. He *heard* it, but Clay rolled them over before he could pay any attention to it. Grade sucked in a breath—the air warm from Clay's mouth—and cursed raggedly as Clay's cock was forced deeper into him. His ass clenched, and the pressure ground against his sandwiched cock made his vision gray out as his brain was hijacked by the flood of pleasure.

"God."

Someone said it. Grade was pretty sure it was him, but he couldn't have sworn to it. He swallowed thickly and grabbed at Clay's shoulders as he wrapped his legs around his waist. Clay chuckled, low and audibly pleased with himself, and pulled away from Grade's mouth. He grabbed a handful of Grade's hair and pulled his head back, throat stretched out bare and tight for wet, tongued kisses that traveled down to his collarbone.

"I thought," Grade said, his voice scratchy in his throat, "this wasn't how we were playing it."

Clay bit him, his teeth sharp and rough against Grade's collarbone, and then pushed himself up on braced arms.

"I changed my mind," he said. From this angle, his grin looked distinctly predatory, and anticipatory goose bumps ran down Grade's arms. He bit his lower lip as Clay slowly pulled out of him, his breath caught in his chest as he waited. "That's the other thing about me. I'm an unpredictable bastard."

He thrust into Grade with one quick stroke. It would have made Grade moan, but the sound stuck in his throat as pleasure flooded under his skin. He dug his fingers into Clay's shoulders, his nails pressed down against an inked skull and bike, respectively, as he lifted his hips to meet the thrust. It felt so good it almost hurt. Or the other way around.

The bed creaked sporadically as each thrust drove Grade down into the mattress. He tightened his legs around Clay's hips, his feet braced against long clenched thighs, and let go of his grip on Clay's shoulder so he could reach down and grab his cock.

Clay made a disapproving sound, but he could sod off. His cock was getting enough attention as Grade's ass clenched and clutched at it.

"God," Grade muttered as he dragged his hand roughly along his cock in jerky, impatient strokes. His hand was slick with come and leftover lube. He could feel the knot of tension in his stomach and thighs pulse in time with each stroke/thrust until it was squeezed down into the cradle of his hips—a hot ache of need that throbbed in time with the soft, rough grunts from Clay's throat.

He was so close. All he needed was a bit... more.

Clay pushed himself up onto his knees and grabbed Grade's hips in both hands, his thumbs hooked over the knob of bone. It left Grade arched helpless back over the bed, his weight braced on his shoulder blades as Clay slammed into him with quick, rough thrusts. Grade lost hold of his cock as his brain tried to ride the swell of pleasure that pushed at him. He twisted his hands into the sheets, cotton bunched between his fingers as he teetered on the edge.

He'd wanted to be fucked, and he'd gotten his wish. Sweat slid under his ass as Clay dragged him up onto his thighs, fingers tight enough to bruise, and came with a shudder and a hot, wet spill inside Grade. The slick feeling inside him made Grade gasp and tighten his legs around the other man, his heels pressed against his ass.

Clay pulled out abruptly and shoved Grade back down onto the bed. He laid a forearm over his stomach to pin him in place and sprawled out, shoulders nudged between his thighs and mouth warm and wet as he wrapped it around Grade's cock.

This time it was Grade who choked out a "hell" as he reached down to tangle his fingers in Clay's hair. He pressed his head back into the pillows as Clay sucked, wet and lewd, at him, his tongue slick and firm against the underside of Grade's cock.

Pleasure backlashed through Grade like a whip as he came, muscles trembling and nerve endings on fire. He came like it was wrung out of him and then sprawled out boneless on the bed, waiting for the sweat to dry.

Clay lay across Grade's legs for a moment, his chin braced on Grade's thigh. It felt… easy. Without any real thought behind it, Grade reached out and brushed Clay's hair back from his face, fingers tangled through the messy curls. Clay leaned into the touch like a cat, eyes closed and body relaxed.

Then a cellphone rang. Clay opened his eyes with a brief flicker of something like regret and rolled off the bed. The scars on the curve of his ass pulled taut, white and raised, as he strode over and grabbed the phone and cigarette packet up from the dresser in one hand.

"Still bad for you," Grade said. "For the record."

Clay ignored that. He checked who was calling as he headed for the balcony.

"I need to get this," he said. "Make yourself decent. Use the shower if you want."

He didn't even look back at Grade.

Now all that felt easy was Grade… and not in a good way.

Grade kicked the tangled sheets off his feet and lay there for a moment. He had never been much good at pouting, though. It made him want to get up and *do* something. Besides, it wasn't like there was any reason to pretend it was more than what it was: stress relief.

He swung his legs over the side of the bed and went to gather his clothes up off the floor. When he picked his jeans up, the weight of them caught him by surprise for a second, and then his phone fell out of the pocket with a hard crack as it hit the wooden floor.

"Shit," he muttered as he grabbed it to check for cracks.

He ran his thumb down the screen, and it flickered to life. There were a dozen messages, all in the last half hour. He didn't recognize the number.

Grade swiped to unlock the phone. Photos. Of Dory, with a split lip and a furious look on her face, up against a metal wall.

The final message was just an address and the instruction to *tell no one.*

Something opened up inside Grade and took everything. All that was left was the hollow rush of panic and the thin, unconvincing reminder that—

I promised her.

Grade swallowed hard, his mouth dry and sour, and then walked over to the balcony. Clay held up a finger to beg another second on the call, then frowned as he took a good look at Grade.

"Hold on," he said to whoever he was talking to. "Grade? What do you—"

Grade grabbed both doors and slammed them shut. On the other side of the glass, Clay stared at him for a moment and then shook his head.

"Don't you fucking dare—" he said as he lunged forward.

He didn't get to finish. Grade quickly locked the doors, and Clay bounced off them like a big pissed-off moth.

Naked pissed-off moth.

Grade took a deep breath as he looked at Clay through the doors.

"Sorry," he said.

Clay smacked his hand on the glass.

"Sorry," Grade said again, and then he fled.

# DIRTY WORK

# CHAPTER TWELVE

**"SHUT THE FUCK UP,"** Clay said as Harry unlocked the balcony doors.

Harry held up both hands, palms out, and pressed his lips together in exaggerated "shut up" as he stepped back into the bedroom. He pointedly didn't look down as Clay stalked into the room and shoved past him.

It was hard to tell if it was the scars or the cock he didn't want to be caught staring at. Clay supposed it didn't matter.

Clay grabbed a pair of jeans out of the laundry and dragged them on. Come was still sticky on his thighs and stomach, but he ignored that.

"What happened?" Harry asked.

"You need the birds and the bees talk right now?" Clay snarled as he dragged an old T-shirt on over his head. He tucked the front of it into his jeans and reached for the shoulder holster hung on the back of the door. "When two men really, really want to fuck—"

"Not that 'what,'" Harry blurted out as he went red about the ears. He rubbed his hand over his face and cleared his throat. "I meant after *that*. On the balcony."

Clay thumbed the code into the gun safe and yanked it open.

"I already told you to shut up, Harry," he said as he pulled out the Beretta semiautomatic. He ran through the checklist on autopilot and slid it into the holster. He turned to give Harry a cold look. "We get on. Don't make me fuck that up."

Harry took a step back and then stopped. He screwed his face into a reluctant grimace and scratched his neck.

"Yeah, but…" he said.

"What the hell do you want?" Clay snarled. He stalked forward and got into Harry's face, close enough that they almost touched. "You want a blow job? Go ask your wife."

"I don't want that," Harry asked. "And that was an odd place to take this. I'm just… you sure you want to be a scary asshole about this?"

Clay grinned, thin and mean.

"If it'll get you to shut up—"

"Not to me," Harry said. "You like the kid."

That was close enough to the bone to cut through the strangled hiss of Clay's temper. He stepped back and grabbed a shirt to pull on over his gun. "He's twenty-six," he said.

Harry shrugged that off.

"I'm just saying—"

Clay ignored him and started for the door. Before he got there, Harry was in front of him.

"I'm just saying," he repeated as he braced his hand against Clay's chest. "From what I've seen, Pulaski is a cold little shit. He's not the type to go off half-cocked. Whatever happened, he had to at least think it wa—aargh."

Clay gripped Harry's hand and bent it back until his thumb touched his forearm. Harry folded at the knees, sweat on his forehead.

"One. Unless I ask you to touch me, don't fucking touch me," Clay said. "Two. I don't care what his reason was for locking me buck-naked on my own balcony. Three. If I want to know what you think, I'll stop telling you to shut up. Are we clear?"

Harry swallowed hard. "Yeah," he said through gritted teeth. "Not my business. I get it."

It would be easy enough to break Harry's wrist. The thought floated through Clay's mind for a second before he abandoned it. He let go instead and stepped around Harry to get to the door.

"Get up," he said. "I need a ride."

He was halfway down the stairs before he heard Harry's footsteps following him. They didn't say anything as they headed out to the car.

That was fine.

Clay climbed into the passenger seat and slouched back, legs stretched out in the footwall. He had a feeling that after tonight Harry wasn't going to worry about what would happen if someone called his bluff anymore. Give him a couple of hours and Clay might regret that.

"Where are we going?" Harry asked as he got into the car.

Clay dropped his head back against the seat and tried to think through the *itch* of his mood. He was pissed off. The thin skin of post-fuck dopamine had been scraped away, and underneath was all raw and twitchy. It *stung*, and Clay's knee-jerk response to that was always to hurt someone else and see how they liked it.

But Harry was annoying, not wrong.

Clay closed his eyes and remembered Grade's face just before the bastard had slammed the doors shut. He'd looked grim and on edge, spooked in the way Clay had seen new recruits on their first tour in the sandbox. And he'd had his phone clutched in one hand, knuckles white against his skin.

"Clay?" Harry poked.

Money was a possibility. Grade had made no secret of the fact he didn't intend to stay in Sweeny, and he needed money to fund the move back. Besides, it wasn't like *Ezra* fucking Clay over. The only thing between Clay and Grade was a tension-relieving fuck. That was a bond that didn't take a lot to break.

More likely, it was a threat. There'd been no dog at the house, so that left the mom, the sister, or the kid.

Either way, it had to be Hadley or Ezra behind it. Hopefully, it was Hadley. Clay didn't want to have to make that choice.

"The Slap," Clay said abruptly enough that Harry started in his seat. He wedged the uncomfortable realization that it would be a choice, not a done deal, to the back of his head. That was something to drown in the good whiskey later. "I need to get some gear and check in with Ezra."

Harry nodded and started the engine. He did a U-turn on the drive while Clay popped the glove compartment open to fish out one of the burners. The radio crackled and then caught a station as Clay tore open a sim card with his teeth.

"Swwwwwweeeeeeee…" the singer wailed.

Clay killed it before he got to the state. "I need to make some calls," he said.

"You're the boss," Harry said as he pulled out onto the road. He pressed his foot down on the gas, and the engine growled as the speedometer nudged up toward eighty. "I got the memo."

Clay checked to see if he cared about that. The hot red static of anger had already started to simmer down to just pissy. His temper had always been a flash in the pan, hot just long enough to do something stupid, cooled down in time that you could regret it.

So maybe a bit.

"So, did I?" he asked as he slotted the card in and booted up the phone. "Fuck up us getting on?"

Harry kept his attention on the road.

"Yeah, well, next time you tell me to roll up a window, I'm going to do it," Harry said. Then he shrugged one shoulder and hung his hand over the steering wheel. His wrist was still welted up from where Arlo had scratched him, and probably still kind of sore from being half-broken... but who was keeping score? "But you were locked on your balcony with your cock hanging out, so I'll cut you some slack."

"Felt like an underachieving Rapunzel," Clay grumbled as he opened the browser to look up the contact details for the nicest hotel in town. "I'll tell you that."

Harry laughed.

"And don't worry about the windows," Clay said as he hit the green icon to make the call. "I'm thinking of giving up smoking."

"Yeah?" Harry said.

Clay leaned his arm against the door frame, phone pressed against his ear.

"Yeah," he said. "Why make someone's day by dying young, right?"

He supposed he could lie to himself about why, but he'd already talked himself down from murdering Grade. That had taken about five minutes. By the time they found him, Clay would be down on one knee with a ring. Or maybe not that far, but... yeah.

Harry was right. He liked the kid.

Who was twenty-six, which was perfectly appropriate.

The call connected. Clay hit 0 repeatedly with his thumb until the system dumped him through to the front desk. It was—

he glanced at the dash briefly to check—after four. Terry should be on shift.

"Hello, this is Cave Lock Spa and Lodge," Terry said, her voice chocolatey smooth. "How can I help you?"

"It's Clay."

"Fuck." The rough edges of her accent broke through, and that was the Terry he knew. "What do you want? I'm at work."

"Yeah, me too," Clay said. "I need to know if someone's staying there. Tall guy, from Lexington. Looks expensive. He's got TJ with him. Or a car that has muffled screams coming from the trunk. Could be either."

There were other hotels. Motels. Flophouses. If Clay came into town to do some bad shit, that's where he'd go. Mouthpiece, though, Mouthpiece looked like someone who liked the nicer things in life. Why else wear a tailored suit to shake down the locals in a shithole like Sweeny?

"I could lose my job," Tracy said. "Our residents expect their privacy."

Clay cocked one leg up, his boot braced against the dash. "They also expect a nice wine list of pharma from you," he pointed out. "You could lose your job for that too."

She hissed out a sigh between her teeth.

"Fine. What's his name?"

"If I knew that, I would have led with it," Clay said. "C'mon, how many assholes can there be in the building?"

"You'd be surprised," she said dryly. "Give me a minute. I haven't seen him, but I'll check with room service."

She put him on hold. Clay pinched the bridge of his nose between his fingers as he listened to a tinny, out of tune piano plink away. He got through two cycles of it before it cut off mid-plink.

"He's here," Tracy said. "Room 631. He checked in last night, asked for a mountain view and ordered creamy pesto shrimp for dinner but skipped breakfast. Are we done?"

"Put me through to him," Clay said. "I need to have a word."

"My job..."

"...is to put callers through to the rooms they ask for," Clay said. "Just tell him I already knew."

She made an annoyed noise, and he had dead air in his ear for a second. When it cleared, Mouthpiece's voice said coldly, "What do you want?"

If they'd had the time, Clay had a list at this point. Since they didn't...

"Meet me and Ezra at the Slap in an hour," he said. "We've got Buchanan. That's who you wanted, isn't it?"

There was the sound of Mouthpiece taking a drink on the other end of the line. Then he cleared his throat.

"That's convenient for you, isn't it?" he said.

"You have no fucking idea," Clay said. "If you think I'm lying, come to the Slap in an hour and prove it."

He hung up and idly flipped the phone in his hand a couple of times. Then he grimaced and made another call, to Deputy Jones.

"I need you to keep an eye out for a shit-heap pickup with an Eddyville sticker on the bumper," Clay said. He racked his brain for a second. "License plate... starts 712 or 713. It stays off the record. I'll make it worth your while."

He hung up and shoved the burner into his pocket. Then he bounced his knee absently, the sound of his heel against the dash loud. After a second, Harry glanced his way.

"Maybe give up the smokes tomorrow," he said. "When you know if there's any reason to or not."

Clay ignored him as they turned out of town and hit the more or less straight run to the Slap.

§

Ezra handed Clay a beer and pulled a chair out from the table with his foot.

"You sure about this?" he asked.

Clay slouched back, one arm hung up over the back of the chair, and watched the front door of the Slap. He rubbed his finger against the scarred wood, over and along the nicks and lines.

"You know whiskey makes me pissy," he said.

Ezra snorted. "Yeah," he said. "Yeah, we all remember that. I mean talking to Nesmith."

"Mouthpiece?"

Ezra winced. "Do you have to?"

"Yes and no," Clay said. He lifted the beer to his mouth and took a swig, one eye still trained on the door. "I had genuinely forgotten his name."

"Why?"

Clay swallowed and wiped his mouth on the back of his hand while he thought about that. "I mean, hard to say. But probably 'cause I was kind of fucked up on coke. Also, I didn't care, so I didn't listen."

"That's my point," Ezra said. He twisted the cap of his beer off and flicked it toward the bar. "What's going to make this meeting different?"

His phone buzzed. He flipped it over to check the message and swore quietly. Clay raised an eyebrow.

"They here?"

Ezra nodded grimly. It looked like the Catfish Mafia was on the premises.

Clay set his bottle of beer down on the table.

"And the difference is," he said as he stood up, "right now, I care."

The doors opened, and Mouthpiece—Nesmith—walked in. He was wearing a different suit, although he'd left the tie back at the Lodge. The collar of his shirt was open, probably to show he meant business. Only two of his men were with him: a skinny blond and the limpy asshole from earlier. The rest…

Clay tucked his tongue into the corner of his mouth as he considered his options. Four around the back. Probably two over at the gas station, up on the roof with long-range rifles. He glanced over toward the window *he'd* have aimed through and gave whoever the sniper was the finger. Ezra grabbed his forearm and squeezed.

"Problem?" Nesmith said as he paused.

"He thinks I'm going to make things worse," Clay said. "To be fair, I got form with that. So…"

Nesmith glanced at Limpy. "Yeah," he said. "I've seen your work. You asked to see me. What do you want?"

Clay put his finger and thumb in his mouth and whistled sharply. After a second, Harry came out of the back with a drum propped up on a trolley. He clunked it down just in front of the table, and it audibly sloshed. Clay slapped his hand on the top of it.

"I already told you. We found Buchanan."

"I'll be the judge of that," Nesmith said. "Open it up."

Harry got to work on that with the same screwdriver Grade had used. While they waited, Clay picked up his beer for a sip.

"So what did he do?" he asked. When Nesmith gave him a look, he nodded at the drum. "Buchanan. Did he kill the wrong guy, fuck the wrong girl? Other way around? Was it just money?"

"Just money?" Nesmith said. "If that's your attitude, maybe the terms of our agreement were too generous to start with."

Ezra cleared his throat. "They were not," he said as he stood up. "Clay, get to the point."

The lid came off. Nesmith looked into the body soup without flinching.

"Where's his head?"

Clay plunged his arm in and groped around until he felt hair. The liquid was warm and thick, slimy despite the thin, bleachy smell, and he tasted bile in the back of his throat as he pushed a bit of arm out of his way. He wasn't going to lie—not to himself—it was absolutely disgusting. He didn't let that show on his face as he pulled Buchanan's head out.

*Stuck in a thumb*, his brain dredged the old rhyme back up and scattered it through his brain in dissonant, rattling tones, *and pulled out a* squelchy *plum*.

Liquid dripped off Clay's arm and splattered on the floor as he turned the head around to face Nesmith. What was left of the face.

There was a pause as everyone stared at it.

"All right," Nesmith said. He gestured for the head to go, and Clay dropped it back into the soup. "You've found Buchanan. We had hoped for him alive."

"Well, I don't think he's getting better," Clay said. He shook the gunk off his arm and sat back down to look at Nesmith. "See, thing is, I know ol' Bit Part Buchanan there fucked up. Why else would you be here."

Ezra nodded at Harry to leave. Then he kicked a chair out from the table for Nesmith.

"It's a good point," he said. "Even if Buchanan was meant to check in after he made the pickup, you'd still have needed a good day to get here. Maybe you'd be rolling into town around now."

"Instead, you beat him here," Clay said. "You checked into the Lodge yesterday. My theory?"

Nesmith sat down. His men stood behind him. "Go on," he said.

"Buchanan robbed you—and by you, I mean Fisher— absolutely fucking blind," Clay said. "Obviously, that's not something you want to get out. People are greedy. The last thing you want to do is give them ideas."

Nesmith reached over the table and took Clay's beer. He took a swig and leaned back in the chair, bottle balanced on his knee.

"So, not something I'd want to confirm to two second-rate thugs from the back end of nowhere," he said. "No offense."

Ezra snorted. "Look, we saw this shit play out before," he said. "With more money and bigger players. The reason you wanted Buchanan alive is that he still had your money. Either he'd transferred it out of your reach or he'd cashed up before he left Lexington. It's probably the latter. Folding money is hard to track. Unless you're the government."

Clay nodded. "True that."

Nesmith drank his beer.

"Even if that were true—"

Limpy made a noise in protest and stepped forward. "Fisher already told us to—"

Nesmith glanced around at him. "Then squeal on me to Fisher," he said wearily. "But don't interrupt me again."

"Or what?" Limpy asked. "I answer to Fisher. Not you. I—"

Nesmith moved slightly and braced his expensively shod heel against Limpy's foot. The expression on his face didn't even change as he applied pressure. Limpy screamed, went a sickly color, and doubled over to dry retch.

"You don't have a leg to stand on," Nesmith said. "Get him out of here."

The blond man grabbed him and dragged him outside, face grim and exasperated. Nesmith watched him go and then turned back to Clay and Ezra. He adjusted his jacket fastidiously.

"Sorry for that," he said. "As I was saying… if that's true, which I haven't confirmed or denied, why did you call me down here to tell me things I already know?"

"If it were true," Clay parroted.

"Exactly," Nesmith said.

For a second, habit made Clay look at Ezra. He got a shrug as the ball was tossed back to him. This was his play, good or bad. Fuck it. Gut instinct had led him astray before, but what the hell else did he have.

"Buchanan wasn't working alone," he said. "He had a woman—an ex-stripper with a shoulder tattoo?"

Nesmith shrugged. "We didn't move in the same circles," he said. "I'm glad he was loved?"

"Well," Clay said. "She's the one who got him killed. Her and her partner. They shot Buchanan in there—" He pointed over his shoulder at the restrooms. "—then set TJ up for it."

"TJ said you did it."

"I didn't."

"That is what you'd say," Nesmith pointed out, "if you had done it."

Clay clenched his jaw on his irritation for a second and took a deep breath. He didn't have time for this, but he needed to get Nesmith on-side.

"Fisher had us checked out," Ezra said. "We might be second-rate, but we aren't amateurs. If we wanted Buchanan dead, we would have waited until he made the next check-in and we weren't the obvious suspects. They told TJ that Clay had set him up to get him to run, and then they called you and told you where to find him. Right?"

"You blamed our neighborhood crooked cop," Clay said. "But I fed you that one. Right?"

Nesmith finally lifted his hand off the gun. He leaned back and absently pressed his thumb into the palm of his hand as he glanced between them.

"It was a woman," he said. "Could have been this Jones, for all I know. OK. So Buchanan stabbed Fisher in the back, ran off with his mistress, and then—I guess—got stabbed in the back himself. That's… tidy."

Clay shook his head. "You'd be surprised how untidy it's got," he said. "But our offer? We give you the mistress and her partner. If anyone knows where that money got to, it's them."

"And in return?"

"Three things," Clay said. "A clean slate for us—"

"That's up to Fisher," Nesmith said immediately. "But I think he'd be amenable."

"And you pull the men you've got watching the motel out of there," Clay said. "You can give me the room number if you're feeling generous."

"What motel?" Nesmith asked calmly, his face unreadable.

"I know Buchanan wasn't at the Lodge, so that leaves the Kettlebottom Motel and the Motel 6 on the road out of town,"

Clay said. "It'll cost me fifty bucks and some time to find out which. I can live with that, but you want this deal? I don't want your people there when I drive up to whichever it is."

Nesmith finished the beer. He set the bottle down on the table and picked up his gun to tuck it away under his jacket.

"That's two," he said. "What's the third? You want me to cut TJ loose?"

Huh. That was awkward. Clay glanced over at Ezra, who shrugged.

"TJ stabbed me," he said as he extended his arm over the table to display the dressing. "He got himself into this; he can get himself out of it."

"What we need is four hours grace," Clay said. "To clean up some loose ends."

"Two hours grace," Nesmith said. He stood up and shot his sleeve back to check the time. "That will give me time to check with Mr. Fisher about the clean slate. He will have his own conditions, of course, but I would put money on one of them being 'keep your mouth shut.' So bear that in mind. That said… I'll call my people off the Kettlebottom. Give it ten minutes and they'll be out of there."

Relief wadded up like gauze in the back of Clay's throat. He coughed and nodded.

"I'll take it from there," he said.

"Good luck," Nesmith said. He paused and then added pointedly, "Because you do *not* get a second chance to let Fisher down."

Nesmith turned and headed out. He stepped fastidiously over the bloody trail that his thug had left behind him. He stopped at the door and looked back.

"Room thirty-four," he said. "Save that fifty for a new pair of boots."

He left. Clay glanced toward the window and gave the sniper a thumbs-up.

"Would you give it a rest?" Ezra said. "You pulled it off. Don't fuck it up now. Go find Pulaski and use him to get to Hadley before Fisher starts asking for bodies on a slab. Oh, and try not to let your cock do the thinking for you."

Clay stood up and pulled his jacket off the back of the chair.

"I don't know what you're talking about," he said. "And make sure Harry's ready when I need him."

The sound of Ezra's snort followed Clay out of the bar. He paused in the parking lot and gave Nesmith's car a sarcastic salute as it reversed out onto the road.

*Room 34 at the Kettlebottom.* Clay headed for Harry's truck. He just hoped to hell that was where Grade had gone, because he had no other ideas.

# DIRTY WORK

# CHAPTER THIRTEEN

**"FIFTY BUCKS FOR** the room," the woman behind the plastic said without looking up from her Kindle. She absently picked at a hangnail on her thumb. "Cash or card?"

"Card." Grade wiped his sweaty hands on his chinos and got his wallet out.

It was habit that made him run the math in his head: how many more hours in Sweeny would those dollars cost him? He didn't begrudge fifty dollars for his sister. If he thought of value gained instead of lost, it was a steal.

He swiped his card in the reader when the woman shoved it through the slot to him. She flipped a page in her book as she waited for the transaction to go through. Once it did, she sighed, put her device down, and reached for a stack of blank cards.

"Room thirty-three or thirty-five," Grade said.

She looked up at him. "Any reason why?" she asked, her nails poised over the rack of plastic slips.

"Yeah," Grade said. "Mine. Can I get one or not?"

The woman pursed her lips and sucked her teeth as she checked the computer. After a minute, she turned her mouth down at the corners.

"It's another fifty," she said. When Grade reached for his card, she tsked at him and rubbed her fingers together. "Cash. Up front."

He stuck the card back in its slot and flicked through his thin stack of bills.

"I've got… twenty-five," he said and put it down on the desk.

"That's nice for you," she said. "I need fifty."

The phone in Grade's pocket felt like it was red hot. He didn't *think* Hadley had eyes and ears on him, but he didn't know for sure. It made the back of his neck itch.

"Twenty-five now, and a hundred when I leave," he said. "Deal?"

She scratched at her temple with a long manicured nail. "How does that work?" she asked. "Do you have the bills stuck up your ass?"

"No. I'm going to turn expensive tricks for a john with a numbers thing," Grade said through gritted teeth. "Just give me the room."

She sniffed and sat back in her chair. "Could have just said you were hooking," she said. "We got a special rate for that."

Grade bounced his heel while she got the card ready.

"Room thirty-three," she said. "Ice is on the ground floor and—"

"I don't care," Grade said. "Stairs?"

She jerked her thumb over her shoulder. Grade stuck the card in his pocket, grabbed the backpack of improvised gear, and headed that way. He got his phone out and checked it as he went up a flight.

There were no new messages—just that last picture of Dory and the flat demand that Hadley had texted an hour ago.

I don't care how you get the money. I get my hundred grand by midnight or I hurt her.

Asshole. Grade clenched his hand around the phone so hard it took a second to let go. The mixture of anger and panic was knotted up in his chest like wire. It made it hard to think. Except, the only thing he could do for Dory was think. Someone like Clay might be able to pull off going in all guns blazing and save the day. Grade would just get them both killed.

Cody would grow up like they had, never knowing the truth.

Bile stung the back of Grade's throat. He forced it back down and headed for the next flight up. By the time he reached the third floor, there were dark patches of sweat under his arms and he could smell himself even more than he had before.

He dropped the bag and fumbled the key out of his pocket. It nearly slid out of his sweaty fingers as he slotted it into the door. Grade pulled it back out and waited for the door to unlock while he tried to look as much like a typical motel resident as possible.

The two guys in the Honda that had been parked in the Dairy Queen were gone, but that just meant they'd moved somewhere else. They still thought Buchanan might be back.

It took three tries before the card finally worked. Grade kicked the door open and dragged his bag inside. It swung half shut behind him, and he left it for now as he took in the room. The walls were a grubby beige, the carpet looked rough and somehow dusty, and the bedspread was bright yellow and pocked with melted cigarette burn holes. It made Grade's skin crawl. He could practically feel the bedbugs behind his ears.

He let himself scrub behind his ears once, with both hands simultaneously, until his skin felt hot and clean. Then Grade put it out of his head as he finally flicked the light on, closed the door, and emptied his backpack onto the floor.

Motels had thin walls. Anyone who'd ever stayed in one could swear to that. Any noise in the other room—sex, soaps, or some asshole playing *Call of Duty* without his headphones at 1:00 a.m.—sounded like it was right in your ear.

Nobody ever thought about how easy it would be for anything *else* to get through those walls. They just believed in walls and the social compact of not going through them. Otherwise, Grade supposed, as he untangled the cord of the power saw, they'd never stay anywhere but at home.

There was also the fact that, in most hotels, there would be someone to kick up a fuss if they heard walls being taken down randomly in the middle of the day. Lucky for Grade, the Kettlebottom wasn't that sort of motel. Even if someone complained, Grade's money was on him being done and gone *before* the woman at the reception desk finished her chapter and could be fucked to come up.

He plugged the saw into a socket, lined it up against the wall, and pulled the trigger. It whined to life, high-pitched and juddering, and the vibration numbed Grade's hands as he cut a lopsided oblong into the wall.

It bothered him more than he liked to admit that it wasn't straight.

One of the pictures—a smiling girl in a field of grass with a random, massive cross behind her—fell off the wall as he worked. It bounced on the carpet, and the glass shattered. Grade made a mental note to add ten bucks to what he owed when he got back down.

Finally, he managed to force the lines to cross. He pulled the saw back and turned it off. Even when the blade stopped, he could still feel the vibration in the bones of his hand. He set it down on the floor, grabbed the hammer, and started to pull chunks of wallpaper and cheap drywall off. Once there was a big enough gap, he dropped the hammer and used his hands.

Blisters stung across the heart of his palm, and his fingertips were dry and scraped up by the time he finished. He resisted the urge to check the time—the deadline ticked down whether he looked or not—and dragged the duct-tape-patched armchair over to climb up on.

Grade balanced one foot on the arm of the chair as he squirmed through the hole he'd made. Bits of the sliced-through board caught at his T-shirt and scraped his stomach. There was a chest of drawers against the wall on the other side. He hit it with his shoulder and hip as he fell into the room.

He pushed himself onto his hands and knees, wiped his face on the back of his arm, and then someone grabbed the back of his neck with a hard hand and dragged him to his feet. Grade squawked out a "fuck" and threw a wild punch.

Clay grabbed his wrist in his free hand. He looked grim, his hair raked back from his face and jaw set.

"Fuck," Grade said again. An uncomfortable squirm of what was—probably—guilt made the back of his throat taste bad. He swallowed it and licked his lips nervously. "I didn't want to—"

Clay gave him a quick, impatient shake to shut him up. Then he pulled him into a rough kiss that scraped stubble over Grade's mouth and pressed his body against Clay's. After a confused second, Grade gave into it. He leaned against the hard planes of lean muscle and shoved both hands into Clay's curls to pull his head closer.

It felt…

He wanted…

Grade didn't know what it was. He felt like he could breathe for the first time since he'd got the text—that he could just stop for a second, for long enough to drink in the taste of Clay's mouth.

It was Clay who broke the kiss. He tilted his head back, away from Grade's instinctive attempt to chase his mouth.

"You could have asked for help," Clay said as he stepped back. "But you couldn't do that, could you? Smart City Boy like you, needing help from some backwoods thug with a GED?"

Grade wiped his nose on the back of his hand. "That's not fair."

Clay put his knuckle under Grade's chin and tilted his head back. "You locked me buck naked on my own balcony," he said. "I don't have to be fair. What are you…? Don't. Don't cry. OK. I'm not that pissed."

Grade wiped his nose again and lifted his chin. "What are you talking about? I don't cry. I'm not ten."

He sniffed and tasted salt on the back of his tongue.

"Yeah," Clay said. He wiped his thumbs under Grade's eyes. "I can see that."

Grade took a breath and felt it wobble in his chest. He turned away and —*fuck sake*— pulled the hem of his T-shirt up to wipe his face. His eyes stung, and for some reason, it felt good. Not great, but better. He couldn't remember the last time he'd cried.

That was a lie. He could. It just wasn't a good memory.

"It's the dust," Grade said. "From the wall."

"Sure," Clay said. He sounded as relieved as Grade did to have a reasonable excuse for the breakdown. "That makes sense. You OK now?"

Grade took a deep breath. He felt it catch in his chest, but nothing new leaked out of him, so…

"Yeah," he said. "Sorry."

He gave his face one last wipe and turned back around. "Look, I screwed up," he said. "I know that, but why would I ask you for help? Why would you want to help us?"

Clay looked pissed but just shook his head.

"That's a fucking sad thing to say," he said. "Jesus Christ, Grade."

That wasn't an answer. Grade let it go, though. After the whole "naked moth" thing, he didn't have the goodwill banked to push it. He sat down on the edge of the bed. It creaked under him, and the smell of old piss and mothballs oozed out of the mattress.

"What are you going to do?" he asked.

"Help," Clay said. "I'm going to help both of us. But that means you have to trust me."

Grade hesitated for a second as he squinted at Clay and tried to work out how he was going to get fucked over. Because he probably was. People were, in general, out for themselves. That's why he got money upfront.

Except he didn't have a lot—any—options right now, and letting Clay in felt a little like kissing him. It made the knot in Grade's chest loosen until he could breathe without choking on the air. So he'd just be surprised when Clay dropped him in it. He'd survive that. He always did.

"OK," he said. "What do you want to know?"

Clay pointed at the wall. "Why the fuck you cut a hole in the wall instead of knocking on the door," he said. "And how much Hadley wants to ransom your sister."

"A hundred grand by midnight. Hadley said that once I had it he'd tell me where to take it," It didn't sound any less an amount of money or any more of a reasonable time frame when you said it aloud instead of reading it in a text. "And there were people outside watching the motel. I didn't want them to see me go in. I don't have the time to explain."

Clay chewed his lower lip.

"A hundred grand?" he said. "That's all."

"Yeah," Grade said bitterly. "Just pocket change."

"Buchanan stole money from the Catfish Mafia," Clay said. He turned on his heel as he talked and looked around the room. "He must have been skimming off the top for years. Me, I'd be fucking thrilled if someone dropped a hundred grand in my lap. But it's not 'run away and live out the rest of your life in Mexico' money, and that's what Buchanan would have needed to do. Someone like Fisher can't let one of his men get away with stealing from him. He'd wait years, decades, to get his own back. A hundred grand isn't enough money to run far enough or hide well enough. It wouldn't be worth the risk for Buchanan."

That did make it sound like a *slightly* smaller amount of cash. Slightly. Grade didn't see how it changed anything, though. It was still more than he had.

"Maybe the rest of the money is in an off-shore account somewhere?" he said. "This was just his run-for-it stash?"

"Then why would Elizabeth have him killed now, in Sweeny?" Clay asked. "If her and Hadley had pulled it off, they would have got $50K each. Why not wait and get the whole haul?"

Grade rubbed his forehead. He could feel the seconds as they ticked away.

"Why did someone steal Buchanan's *shoes*?" he asked. "People do stuff that makes no sense all the time. Maybe she knows where the rest of the money is?"

That made Clay nod reluctantly. He chewed on the side of his thumbnail as he thought it through. "So Hadley gets his $50K, and she gets the rest of the money once the heat's died down," he said. "Hell, once everyone, including Fisher, knows Buchanan is dead, there won't be any heat. No one would look for her. Does this place look like a guy has stayed in it?"

The sudden question caught Grade by surprise. It dislodged the itch of *something* that had nudged at him while Clay talked through Hadley and Elizabeth's plan. He tried to catch the tail of it, but it was gone.

"Um." He looked around the room. There was a dirty tissue with lipstick blots on it on the dresser and a spray of setting powder on the mirror. The clothes in the wardrobe were wrinkled and were mostly dresses and leggings. A few pairs of jeans, but… "No. And how long was Buchanan supposed to have been in town?"

Clay held up a finger. He went over to the dresser and picked up the phone.

"Hey, Jasmine," he said. "How long has thirty-four been occupied?"

He listened for a second.

"And that's one person. Huh. You ever seen anyone else here? OK. Thanks."

He dropped the phone back in the cradle. "Buchanan booked the room, but it was a woman who stayed here. She came and went unpredictably, but she's rented this room for a month," he said. "Same amount of time that Hadley's been in town. So she had the money, and the plan was for Buchanan to just swing through—first new stop on his usual route, so a planned disruption—grab her, and disappear. Well, that was his plan. Meanwhile, Elizabeth planned to kill him and then her and Hadley split the cash. Except now she's in the hospital, and Hadley can't get the money until Fisher's men leave town. Makes sense."

Grade shook his head. "No," he said.

"Makes sense to me," Clay said. "Maybe I'm just too dumb to keep up, City Boy."

Grade winced. "Don't," he said.

"It was a joke. I'm a lot of things," Clay said. "Insecure ain't one of them."

That was a lie. Grade had seen the tension on Clay when he'd flashed his scars and the way he'd relaxed when Grade hadn't flinched. Some things didn't need to be poked at, though. Not when you already had bad news to deliver.

"This was just the first place I could think of to look. Hadley doesn't *know* where the money is," Grade said. "It's my job to find it… before he starts cutting my sister's fingers off."

Grade's voice cracked, and the taste of salt bloomed in the back of his throat again. He sniffed and pressed his thumb hard against his upper lip until it died away again. He didn't know what was wrong with him. Anger was useful. Self-pity wasn't.

"It's OK," Clay said. He put a hand on Grade's shoulder and squeezed. "We don't need to find the money."

"Yeah," Grade said. "If you're going to suggest I tap my dad's stash? Meth's gotten cheaper since then, and he's also dead, and I have no idea where they dumped his body. I already told Hadley that."

Clay rubbed his thumb over the nape of Grade's neck.

"We don't *need* the money; all we need is Hadley to *think* we've found it," he said. "Do you trust me?"

"I… I met you yesterday."

"Do you trust me?"

"You were standing over a corpse taking a piss."

Clay grinned and pulled Grade's head down until their foreheads touched. "And you trust me."

This time it wasn't a question. It didn't need to be. Grade needed his head examined—because everything he'd just said was true—but he didn't need that to be a question.

"I trust you," Grade admitted.

"Text him back," Clay said. "Tell him you have the money."

Grade reached for his phone even as he shook his head. "What if he knows I'm lying?" he asked, his fingers clenched around the phone so tightly it felt like he had squeezed the sweat out of his palms. "He's got my sister. She'll already have pissed him off. You've met her. He could hurt her. I won't... I'm the big brother. I might be a shit one, but it's my job to protect her, to keep her safe."

Clay cupped the side of Grade's face in his hand. "Tell Hadley you've found the money, ask him where he wants to meet you, and then I'll kill him for you. If he doesn't know where the money is, no one will care if he's dead."

# DIRTY WORK

# CHAPTER FOURTEEN

**NOTHING WAS EVER** quite that simple, of course.

Clay might not have a lot of respect for some of Hadley's recent choices, but the man wasn't stupid. He'd pulled the wool over all their eyes, one way or another, and made Clay look like a fucking amateur once already. He wasn't going to get the chance to do it again.

"You got this?" he asked Grade as he held out the bait-bag. There was a couple of grand in cash on top, fresh out of the cash machine. It still had that new money smell of hot paper and fresh ink. "All I need you to do is keep his attention on you for as long as possible."

Grade took the bag and hefted it reluctantly in his hands. The run-down motel room, a woman's scant life hung up on unpadded hangers, felt like the wrong background for the scene.

"This is going to get us all killed," he said.

"That's right," Clay said. He cupped the back of Grade's neck in one hand and gave him a light shake. "Stay positive."

Grade pulled a face but didn't squirm away. He took a deep breath.

"It's too late to change the plan now, anyhow," he said. "I already told Hadley I have the money."

Something raw throbbed down in the folds of Clay's brain. He could feel it, like a scab picked off an old cut. How many times had he given this pep talk to an asset or a collaborator before he sent them into a setup?

"Your sister is going to be fine," he told Grade. The words felt weird in his mouth, like someone else had the steering wheel and he just got to watch. "I got this."

It *had* been true more often than not. Clay was good at his job. The rest of his life might be a hot mess navigated by pills and not giving a fuck, but give him a gun and an objective and he was solid. Not always, though.

The woman was screaming so hard the corners of her mouth had split. She had bloody rags and straps clutched in her arms.

Just rags. Clay grabbed Ezra's wrist as Ezra dragged him away from the fire and dug his fingers in. He didn't want— couldn't afford—to let his brain map all those bits together.

The boy was gone. That was all.

Clay rubbed his side absently as the scar tissue convulsed with an itch that dug down between his ribs. This was a job. It wouldn't help to tell Grade that this was his best chance to get his sister back but that didn't mean it would work. Grade already knew that; he wasn't stupid.

"Ready?" Clay asked.

Grade hesitated for a second. Then he suddenly leaned in, one hand twisted in Clay's T-shirt, and pressed a quick, breathy kiss on Clay's mouth. Grade was strung so tight that Clay could feel the tension against his lips like a plucked wire. That was not a first either, but it *felt* like one somehow.

"If I die, do not bury me in Sweeny," Grade said. He stepped back and gave Clay a tight, uneasy smile. "Just in case."

Sure," Clay said. "Too good even in death to hang out with us."

"Yeah," Grade said. "That's right."

He swung the bag onto his shoulder and lifted his phone off the dresser. Hadley hadn't texted again since he'd sent the address for the drop. Cave Lock Dam. The same place that Arlo's dad had taken TJ and, Clay supposed, Elizabeth once upon a time.

"You know, in LA, there are scenic places to do this sort of thing," Grade said. "Near pho restaurants. Do crime *and* have a nice meal. Practically a date."

Clay stepped behind Grade and gave him a shove toward the door. "Go," he said. "When we get out of this, I'll *make* you pho."

"A nice meal," Grade said over his shoulder. "Not food poisoning."

"I'm a good cook," Clay called after him as Grade closed the door behind him. It was true. He didn't usually cook for his hookups—they were there for a hot mess and a wild ride, not dinner, and he was OK with that—but Ezra's kids never complained.

His brain considered that and decided the appropriate response was another highlight reel of his greatest fuckup.

The music was turned up so loud that it sounded like it filled the fucking desert. Taylor Swift. It was a pirated copy, pulled down off YouTube, and the sound was flat and tinny. Who cared. It was turned up as high as the stereo went, and Ezra was hung out the passenger window, drunk and merry, as he sang along to someone else's screwed-up love life.

It made a nice change.

Clay took a swig of vodka from a water bottle. He wasn't drunk, just loose.

Ahead, he saw someone he knew run up to the road, arms in the air as they waved him down.

Someone he knew.

Clay snorted as he grabbed his jacket and shrugged it on. Yeah, that was typical. His brain tried to play the hard man on him, filled his mouth with the taste of vodka and the grit of sand, but pussied out when it came to the money shot.

Khalid.

His name was Khalid.

Clay took the stairs down. He got to the parking lot just in time to watch his car drive away. A second later, Harry pulled out of the Dairy Queen, squashed into Lanie's Nissan Juke, and merged in a couple of cars back.

It would be fine. Harry knew how to tail a car as well as Clay did. He'd worked for the sheriff's department for five years before he'd been "managed out."

Clay got into Harry's SUV. He reached for his cigarettes and had one in his fingers before he remembered his good intentions.

Shit.

He fiddled with a slim white cylinder absently as he put in a call to Deputy Jones on his burner and slid the car into drive. The phone rang twice before Jones finally picked up.

His voice muttered something tinny and crackle-filled. Clay leaned over, one hand still on the wheel, and put him on speaker.

"… owe me," Jones said. "I had to call in favors for this one."

Clay rolled his eyes but kept his voice low and easy. "And I appreciate it," he said. Jones had a wife and went to a very evangelical church. He definitely wouldn't identify as anywhere on the spectrum of liking men, but he got flustered when Clay went slow and let the Louisiana thicken in his voice. It could be useful. "You never let us down, Jones. Now, speaking of, have you got anything for me?"

"The full license plate and registration." Jones preened audibly. "It's registered to Raymond Guthrie, whose last residence was in the State Penitentiary. I've got an official BOLO out on it with the boys. I told them it was some guy who'd been hassling my daughter, and I wanted to have words. If the sheriff finds out about this, I could get an official reprimand. So you owe me."

"I know," Clay said. "You want anything, you just ask, and we can work something out."

Jones grunted in satisfaction, as if Clay had promised him something concrete instead of fuck all.

"I'll let you know if we get a hit," he said.

"Good," Clay said. "It should be on the road sometime in the next thirty minutes. Oh, and one more thing… remember I asked you to pull up the file on that ex-con we hired? Hadley Short. There was no criminal background there, right? He just threw the wrong punch at the wrong time."

"Yeah," Jones said. "That's what it looked like. Why?"

"Just making sure," Clay said.

He hung up.

So Hadley had gone into prison a chump with a good right hook, but he'd come out a kidnapper and murderer—in three years. People did what they had to survive in prison, but if Hadley had gotten in with that crowd, then Guthrie wouldn't have buddied up to him. Clay's old sergeant had plans for life after parole. Plans that would probably land him back in jail, knowing him, but he wasn't going to risk them hanging out with amateurs. And he'd given Clay the heads-up on what sort of jobs the guy was looking for.

It didn't make sense.

Clay absently snapped the smoke he'd been fiddling with in half. He huffed in annoyance and lowered the window to toss the two bits into the undergrowth. People didn't always make sense; that was just the way the world worked.

He was behaving like Grade, obsessed over who stole Buchanan's shoes.

Yes, his brain went, now we're getting it.

Clay waited for more, but he got nothing, just the dopamine dump of a solved puzzle. Except he *hadn't* solved it. He wasn't even sure what the puzzle was. Apparently, that didn't matter. Something in his head thought he'd gotten it, and that was good enough for it.

He rolled his head from one side to the other and reached for the pills in the door. They usually helped him chivvy his brain cells into something like an orderly line. Except it wasn't his car, *and* he'd run out.

Great. Clay grimaced to himself as he took a left onto Grade's street. The Dodge was still parked outside, ripe grape purple in the sun, and there was a deputy's car parked in front of it. Habit made Clay straighten up and focus forward, like a man with nothing to hide. Even though, for once, it was true.

His phone rang suddenly. Clay checked his mirror to make sure there was no one behind the wheel of the patrol car and grabbed the phone.

"You got me," he said. "What you want?"

"Spotted the pickup," Jones said. "You know the Gallagher's hunting plot off the Wildcat?"

"No," Clay said. "I don't hunt, and I don't do trees as landmarks. So with that in mind, what am I looking for?"

Jones blew air out between his lips as if this was a tough question.

"OK, it's an old mining road off the Wildcat," Jones said. "It's after that rock the kids painted blue last year and before the road cuts over the river. If you turn and about ten minutes up, you see an old gray stone building with no roof, you're on the right road. It's the old Hall Company Store."

Clay raised his eyebrows, hit the gas, and spun the steering wheel to do a U-turn over the thin strip of dirt and grass down the median of the road.

"Hall?" he said. "Like Arlo Hall?"

"Yeah. His great-grandfather or something used to run it," Jones said. "Story is he shorted the miners on goods, and one night they came and burned it out. Sounds about right for that family."

It sounded to Clay like the sort of place Elizabeth Hall might suggest her co-conspirator use if he needed somewhere to lie low. Or hold a girl hostage. It would work for either.

"Want me to have someone pull him over?" Jones asked.

"No," Clay said. "No need. Thanks."

He hung up and pressed his foot down on the gas pedal as he headed up the mountain.

Most of the paint had worn off the rock. It was just splattered with gobs of color now, but it was still easy enough to pick out from the plain gray rocks around it. Clay eased his speed down as he cruised past it, on the lookout for the next turn.

The first one he came to looked more like a dirt track than a road. The concrete had cracked and broken up down the middle, only a zipper line of solid gray left on either side to keep the grass and shrubs at bay. Clay cursed under his breath as he drove along it until he saw the old stone building ahead, half-reclaimed by the woods already. Vines crawled up and in through broken windows, and the slate-roof had buckled and broken to let the tree inside stick its head out.

Clay drove on past it. He pushed the SUV as far up the road as he could get, until even the thin strips of gray on either side broke down and it was just mud and grass under the wheels. Far enough, hopefully. He parked and climbed down. Mud squelched under his boots as he cut through the trees on his way back down toward the back of the old store.

He pulled his gun, familiar and heavy in his hand, as he ghosted silently from log to dense bed of moss and back again. It wasn't likely that Hadley would do a sweep of the area, but old habits died hard.

Lucky enough, otherwise Clay would have missed the first tripwire. Pulled tight along an open patch of ground, nearly hidden in the mulch, it was just a glimmer of sunlight that gave it away. Clay crouched down and ran a finger under it as he traced it back to the thin green plastic box discreetly tucked against the base of the stone wall, camouflaged in the long grass.

It was an innocuous enough little box, but Clay had encountered them before. It was a Serbian MRUD, an anti-personnel mine that would have shredded Clay's legs down to the bone if he'd triggered it.

He grimaced. Death wish or not, that would have been a bad way to go.

Clay positioned himself to the side of the device—just in case—and pulled a pocket knife out of his boot to cut the wires. How the hell had someone like Hadley got his hands on kit like this? And why?

His brain winked at him: *You know.*

Except he didn't. Clay growled under his breath as he pushed himself back to his feet and made his way carefully around the edge of the building. The front door had been replaced with a heavy metal door bolted shut with a padlock. Clay could have picked it, if he took the time.

Instead, he stepped to the side and smashed one of the already cracked and grimy windows with the butt of his gun. As the glass broke, he heard a muffled scream from inside. He booted the worm-riddled wooden frame out of his way and climbed in.

The old Hall store smelled like skunk, something dead, and gun oil. In addition to the Serbian mines outside, Hadley—Clay *felt* his brain nudge at him—had a small but effective armory set up in the old building: shotguns and rifles, boxes of ammo. He was set for a siege.

Or maybe this had been Buchanan's stockpile? At some point, Elizabeth and Buchanan had been in on this together. He could have stocked this place up in case their plan went south and Fisher's men caught up with them. Or so it would be ready for them to head down to Mexico. There were plenty of places to get over the border without anyone checking what shit you had with you. More if you knew whose palms to grease, and Buchanan would have.

The scrape of chair legs on the old concrete floor and choked yelps reminded Clay that he could get those answers later. Right now, he wanted to pull Hadley's leverage out from under him.

He found Dory tied to a chair with a tarp thrown over her. She was gagged and blindfolded with oil-stained old rags that dug into her skin. The knots were yanked tight at the back of her head, her hair tangled in with them.

"Dory," Clay said as he tried the knots with his fingers. She whimpered as his attempt to untie them pulled on her hair. "Your brother sent me. We met earlier."

She squirmed furiously in the chair and twisted her head around toward him. He couldn't make her out through the gag shoved in her mouth, but from the tone of it, nothing she said was complimentary.

"I'm here to get you out," Clay said. He gave up on untying the gag and pulled his pocket knife again. The flat of the blade kissed her cheek as he slid it up under the twisted cotton, and she went very still. The only movement was her hands as she clenched them into fists on the arms of the chair. Clay cut the gag free and left her to spit it out while he got to work on the blindfold. It was cut halfway through when he heard the death-rattle groan of the pickup as it pulled up outside. "Shit."

Dory turned her head blindly toward the noise. "Is that him?" she asked. Her voice was thick and dry. She stopped to swallow and tried again. "Why is he back? He said he'd be gone for a while."

"Something went wrong," Clay said easily. "Stick the gag back in your mouth and play along."

He ignored her moan of protest as he threw the tarp back over her. Then he loped back to the front of the store and tucked himself into the shadows there.

The padlock rattled on the other side of the door—someone cursed, a thick angry sound—and then it finally clicked open. Hadley dragged Grade, bag still clutched in his arms, inside.

"You lying redneck piece of shit," Hadley ranted. He pressed his gun up under Grade's jaw, dug deeply enough into the soft skin that Grade had to cock his head back and to the side to escape it. "Did you tell them I was here?"

Grade pulled an annoyed face. "If I did," he said, "would they be trying to kill me?"

"You're an annoying little prick," Hadley said. "I would."

He drew the gun back and punched Grade in the side of the face with it. Grade yelped and went down onto his knees. Blood dripped between his fingers and onto the floor as he cupped his mouth.

"Stay down," Hadley said. "Or I'll put you down for good."

Clay cleared his throat.

Hadley spun around and staggered backward. He swung his gun up, but Clay grabbed his wrist before he could aim it. He broke Hadley's thumb with a sharp jerk and caught the gun as it dropped. He tucked it into the waistband of his jeans and pressed the muzzle of his gun against Hadley's forehead.

"I could say the same to you," he said. "Grade? You OK?"

Grade spat onto the dirty concrete and nodded. "I'll live."

Hadley snorted out a chuckle as he skinned his lips back in a grin. Clay had to admit, from this side of it, that was off-putting.

"Not for long, though," Hadley said. "You know what? It's almost fucking worth it."

Clay was going to ask "What?" but then he heard the other cars pull up outside. He grabbed Hadley by the collar, gun slid around to press against his temple, and dragged him over to the window to look out.

Three black Lexus sedans. None of them belonged to Harry or Ezra.

Fuck.

Doors opened and Nesmith's men piled out, suit jackets stripped off and Kevlar cinched over their shirts. Submachine guns were cradled in the crook of their arms, and Limpy, one foot strapped up in a hospital walking cast, dangled a brace of grenades from one hand as he got out of the back of one of the sedans.

"Fucking Nesmith couldn't see what was right in front of him," Limpy yelled as he hobbled forward. "But I did. Some fucking Dashiell Hammett bullshit about two-timing whores and bartenders. Then you head straight up here, Traynor. What, do you get a cut? Is that why you tried to tell us Buchanan was dead?"

What?

Buchanan was…

"It wasn't Buchanan who got shot," Grade said.

Of course not. Clay had all the pieces already; his brain had just played shuffleboard with them. But here they were now, all laid out, and how the fuck had he missed it the first time?

"Of course it wasn't," Clay said. He looked at Hadley, who grinned at him. "Because you're Buchanan."

The moment of realization was shattered as a burst of gunfire strafed the front of the building.

"You've got five minutes," Limpy said. "Come out or we come in."

# CHAPTER FIFTEEN

**DORY'S NAILS WERE** broken down to the quick. What was left of the red resin polish made her fingers look mutilated. They could have been. Grade tried not to think about it as he unlocked the cuffs. It helped that Dory was already on his case.

"So you just happened to have a handcuff key on you?" she asked, her voice prickly with judgment. "Just hanging out on your keyring."

"Where else would I put it?" Grade twisted the key, and the metal ring clicked open on Dory's right hand. Behind them, Clay had Hadley… Buchanan… pinned up against the wall as he choked the truth out of him. Or as close to it as you could get with the time limit they had. "It's a key. I put it on the key ring."

"Don't try and be smart," Dory said. "Just because you skipped fourth grade—"

"And sixth grade."

She ignored the correction. "It doesn't make you smart; it just makes you clever."

"It's the same thing."

Dory sniffed. "Someone smart would know it isn't," she said flatly as he freed her other wrist. She shook her hands out and reached up to rub her cheeks and behind her ears where the gag had left lines creased into her skin. "Never mind someone who played as much D&D as you did."

Grade sat back on his heels and looked up at her. Of the two of them, she looked more like their dad. The same blue eyes, the same easy way with people… when she wanted. The same nasty streak when she didn't. It made people think she was tough. They didn't know the half of it.

"Did he hurt you?" he asked. "Buchanan."

"I know who you meant," she said. "Who else would I think it was? Santa?"

"That's not an answer. Did he hurt you?"

She shook her head. "No."

"Would you tell me if he did?"

The corners of Dory's mouth, chafed raw red by the gag, tweaked up in a brief, tight smile. "No. But he didn't."

Grade took her hands in his and squeezed. "I'm sorry," he said. "I'll get you out of this."

She nodded. "I know." Dory waited a minute and then pulled her hands back. "And then you find somewhere else to live."

Yeah. Grade supposed that was fair enough. He nodded.

"Same as last time," he told her. "The minute you get a chance, you run and don't look back."

She pressed her lips into a thin white line and nodded. Then she lurched forward and wrapped her arms around Grade's neck. Her nose pressed awkwardly against his ear as she hugged him.

"Asshole," she said.

"Yeah."

She sniffed. Her knuckles dug into his shoulders. "Don't spoil our thing."

He pried himself free, tucked a loose tangle of blonde hair behind her ear with a gentle pat, and headed over to Clay. Time to find out how much of a liar he'd just made of himself.

Buchanan's wrist had started to swell, the skin shiny and red as it stretched out like a water balloon. He cradled it against his chest.

"He looked like me," Buchanan said with a dismissive one-shouldered shrug. "Betsy used to take messages in and out of prison for Fisher. One day she saw Hadley. It was all her idea, this part. Everything else was in place. We had the money and the retirement plans, but we knew that we'd never be able to rest easy if Fisher was after us."

Clay nodded. "But if you gave him a corpse to trawl for trout with—"

"He did that once," Buchanan said. "But yeah, that's the gist of it. So Elizabeth 'got to know' Hadley, convinced the poor sap he was in love with her. He was desperate for something to make the last few years worth it, and here it was, wrapped up nice for him. He hadn't wasted thirty-six months of his life; he'd just been waiting for a beautiful ex-stripper who wanted to turn her life around. When he got out, she talked him out of coming down here, convinced him that she wanted to get away from me and that the two of them just needed to get some money for a fresh start. Oh, and that he needed to get sober—to buy us some time. So she used my credit card to check him into a nice expensive rehab, and I came down here and took his place. Trust me, you got the better end of that deal."

"And Fisher didn't miss you?" Clay asked.

"I told you, I was in rehab. At least, as far as the rehab and my credit card company were concerned, I was," Buchanan said. "When I didn't have a shift for a couple of days, I'd fly up and keep things ticking over. Me and Elizabeth wired money to off-shore accounts and cashed-up some NFTs for mad money until we got to where we were going. Then she sprang Hadley, dressed him up nice in one of my suits, and brought him down here to rob you two blind. And I shot him."

"In the face," Grade said. "Because you looked alike, but not identical. Someone would have told you apart, but between dead and partially disfigured... no one expected too much."

Buchanan nodded. He tilted his head back to rest against the wall. "It was perfect. Until you fucked us up, Cleaner."

Grade nodded. "Because the last thing you wanted was for me to make the body disappear. The whole point was for Fisher to be satisfied you were dead, not off somewhere with his money. One question?"

"Not the time," Buchanan said.

Grade ignored him. "Why did you take his shoes? It's been bothering me."

Buchanan rubbed his finger over his eye and grimaced. "Hadley had bad feet. He turned up for the meet in a nice suit and a pair of sneakers. It would have been the first thing that prick Nesmith would have noticed. That was the first thing that didn't go to plan, and after that it was like dominos," Buchanan said. "One thing after another started to go wrong. From Elizabeth's idiot cousin working out something was going on to Nesmith getting here ahead of schedule. I was like that little boy at the dyke, plugging one leak after another. It worked, though. End of the day, Fisher thinks Buchanan is dead and I'm free and clear. Except..."

"Elizabeth had the money," Clay said.

Buchanan looked sour as he nodded. Then he pointed with his chin at Grade. "I figured that Pulaski there owed me, and besides, I knew about his dad. Pulaski doted on his kids. Even if he'd had to go dark, he'd have left them provided for. So if he couldn't find my cash, he could tap his dad's stash. Except that

mouth-breather, Sloane, somehow worked it out, and he turned
up at the pickup. I walked into a fucking trap, and for what, three
grand and all the tourist attraction leaflets you could grab? I
guess Junior here doesn't love having a stripper for a sister..."

Clay slapped him lightly on the side of the head with his
gun. It made a hollow clunk noise of metal on bone, and
Buchanan flinched back.

"Yeah, yeah, you would have got away with it if it wasn't for
us meddling assholes," Clay said. "But you didn't, and now
we're all fucked. Stay there, or I'll break your other hand.
Grade?"

He cocked his head for Grade to follow him and pulled him
over into the corner of the room. Grade snuck a glance out one of
the grimy windows. The men outside stood around casually—as
casually as anyone in Kevlar vests and carrying submachine guns
could stand—as if they had nothing better to do.

"What are they waiting for?" he asked. "Do they think we
have an army in here?"

Clay pulled a hair tie out of the pocket of his jacket and
scraped his hair back into a rough tail. He snapped the elastic
around the stumpy knot twice.

"They want Buchanan alive," he said. "At least... for a while.
Did you see Harry out there?"

Grade had, but it wasn't exactly good news. "Fisher's men
drove him off the road. They must have recognized him. He
looked OK, but..."

No cavalry on the way, then. Clay rubbed his thumb over his
temple.

"How much were you bluffing at the house earlier?" he
asked.

Grade dragged his attention away from the men outside. "When we—"

"Buchanan's house," Clay said. "Can you use a gun?"

Grade hesitated for a second as he *felt* the flop sweat break on him. He rubbed his sweaty palms against his thighs.

"Yeah," he said. "Dory's a better shot, but we can both shoot. Dad…"

Clay glanced around at Dory, who stood in the middle of the room, arms wrapped around herself.

"That was sexist," Clay acknowledged. "I shouldn't have assumed she couldn't. Can she pull herself together enough to be useful?"

Grade shrugged. "Yeah," he said. "She'll feel better if she has something to do."

Another burst of gunfire hammered the stone walls. Two bullets smashed through the old glass windows and buried themselves in the counter.

"You've got sixty seconds," the man Grade assumed was Sloane yelled. "Play it smart and nobody has to die."

Grade knew that was a lie, but… He looked over at Dory again and then turned to Clay.

"She's not been involved in any of this," he said. "If we give them Buchanan, maybe they'd let her go?"

Clay shook his head. "We told them Buchanan had a partner, a stripper who came from here. Elizabeth isn't here, she's still in surgery at the hospital, but—"

"My stripper sister is," Grade said.

"By the time they believed she wasn't involved," Clay said. "They'd have to kill her anyhow."

There was a point where it didn't matter how much someone *swore* they'd not tell anyone what you'd done, the hospital would snitch for them when they turned up in the ER. Grade knew that math. He'd seen it happen often enough—and cleaned up after it too.

It should bother him more. It just didn't, though. All those people had brothers or sisters or someone who'd miss them. But they weren't *his* sister, and that was the difference.

"So, what's the plan?" he asked.

Clay grabbed a sawed-off shotgun from the stockpile of weapons. He cracked it open to check the ammo and made a satisfied sound that it was loaded.

"The three of you stay in here and keep their attention," he said. "Just keep shooting. Don't worry about what you aim at or how much ammo you have left. They're going to toss flash-bangs in. Just keep shooting. Doesn't matter if you hit anything, as long as it isn't your sister."

"Three of us?" Grade asked dubiously. He glanced at Buchanan. "You trust him?"

Clay snorted. "No," he said flatly. "But his back is against the wall, and he's more use with a gun in his hand than hogtied and underfoot."

"And you?" Grade asked. "What are you going to do?"

Clay braced the shotgun against his hip. "I'm going to go out there and kill them when they aren't looking," he said. "You got that?"

"I don't know if that counts as a plan," Grade said.

"It's what we've got," Clay said. He cupped his hand around the back of Grade's neck and stroked his cheek with a calloused thumb. "What would you do if I said I loved you, City Boy?"

Grade pulled away. He ignored the dumb little sigh that trembled just behind his heart. It was drunk.

"Tell you I don't do that," he said. "Love. Relationships. I'm not wired like that."

Clay winked at him as he backed away. "And I didn't say it," he said. "Don't get killed. I do want to fuck you later."

He turned and jogged away toward the back of the store.

They had about fifteen seconds to get ready if the count Grade had kept in his mind was accurate.

§

It turned out he was two seconds slow.

The heavy metal cylinders of the grenades smashed through windows and bounced off the floors. Grade wrapped his arm around Dory's head, over her ears, and squeezed his own eyes shut. He felt the heat against his back as they went off, and the bang rattled his skull and jabbed hot nails into his ears. It hurt enough to make him gag and the back of his throat sour with bile.

Dory screamed. He could see it, but he couldn't hear it over the staticky whine that bounced from ear to ear. Grade had been nearby when one went off before, but not this close. Near the door, Buchanan had dropped his shotgun and was slapping frantically at his chest and shoulders as the cheap fabric of his hoodie smoldered.

It didn't matter. Grade worked his jaw from one side to the other to make his ears pop—it didn't help—and reminded himself of the stakes. Better deaf than dead. He grabbed a gun from the case and nearly fumbled it as his hand swam, but he managed to hang onto it.

"Just pull the trigger," he yelled at Dory as he shoved a rifle into her hands. "Make them jump."

Dory shook her head and blinked at Grade with watery eyes. "What if I shoot him?" she mouthed. "Clay's out there."

"Try not to," Grade said.

He grabbed a pistol and a couple of magazines, then crawled in a more or less straight line to the window. Sloane stood in front of the car, waiting expectantly, while the rest of his men leaned against hoods and joked with each other. When no one came out, Sloane's expression soured, and he waved his arm to get everyone's attention.

Grade rested his hands on the broad scarred window ledge— decades of paint scored into the wood—and squinted through the sights at Sloane's head. Clay said it didn't matter what they hit, but that didn't mean they couldn't try.

He squeezed his eyes shut as he pulled the trigger. The bang as the gun fired felt like someone had jabbed nails into his abused eardrums. He clenched his jaw and fired again, and bullets sprayed over the ground, the men, and the cars. When the gun clicked on empty, he grabbed for one of the magazines he'd shoved in his pocket.

Next to him, Dory was slightly more restrained. She squinted and fired with patient, machine-like regularity, bullets stitched in a row of divots along the ground. Neither of them hit much else as the men instinctively scattered for cover.

Buchanan, shirt singed and scarred, grabbed the grenades as they spewed smoke and lobbed them back outside. The area in front of the store filled with smoke and movement, the flash of gunfire bright through the gray layers as the Catfish Mafia remembered they were also armed.

In the middle of it, Sloane yelled in frustration as he grabbed a man by the straps of his bulletproof vest and shoved him toward the store.

"G-t—th—e!" he yelled. His voice crackled in and out of muffled audibility. "There's—two of—m."

In the whited-out corner of Grade's peripheral vision—still compromised by the stun grenade—he saw Clay ghost out of the smoke and smash the butt of his shotgun into the back of the man's head. The man pitched forward like someone had cut his strings. Another of Sloane's men turned and raised his gun. Clay stepped forward and shoved the gun to the side with his forearm, so the stutter of bullets shattered the windows of the nearby cars. He pressed the shotgun flush against the man's shoulder and fired. Blood and bone fragments sprayed out as the man's shoulder blade was pulverized. While the man folded at the knees, one hand clutched to his shoulder, Clay grabbed him by the collar and spun him around to use as a shield.

"Grade!" Dory whispered. She shoved at his arm for his attention and mouthed her question exaggeratedly. "Why did you stop shooting?"

"Shit," Grade muttered. "Sorry."

He pulled the trigger on an empty magazine. Habit made him try it again, as if it was a remote with a half-dead battery. Then he dropped it and crouched down to scrabble for another on the floor, still half-obscured by the acrid chemical smoke from the grenade.

Dory screamed suddenly and scrambled back from the window just before one of the cars slammed into it and halfway through. The front of the car was smashed, the hood crumpled, and windshield shattered inwards from impact. Broken chunks of old mountain stone fouled the wheels and jammed it in place as the engine screamed and leaked steam.

"Shit. Shit. Shit."

Grade fumbled with the shotgun he'd grabbed as he tried to look for the trigger and scramble backward at the same time. The warped driver's side door was shouldered open from the inside, and Sloane scrambled awkwardly out.

He braced himself against the car as he pointed a submachine gun at Grade's head.

"I remember you," he said, his voice distorted like the bass on a low-end speaker. Grade had to struggle to hear him. "The pretty boy."

He winked and raised his voice.

"Gun—down!" he yelled. It should have helped, but it made static burst in Grade's ears like popping candy. He got the gist, though, as Sloane limped forward, kicked the shotgun away, and braced a plastic boot against Grade's chest. "Or I'll blow— boyfriend a new—see how you like him then. One! —! Th—"

He didn't get to finish the count. The shotgun blast hit Sloane in the stomach and knocked him off his feet. He slammed back into the wrecked car and then sprawled there as he wheezed. The vest had taken most of the impact, but not all. Blood bloomed on his shoulders and stomach where buckshot had gone under the Kevlar shield or through the straps.

Buchanan, shotgun clumsily braced on his broken wrist, stumbled forward over the smashed down wall. He offered his good hand to Grade.

"I saved your life," he said. "How about you help me get out of here? We can call it even."

§

It was over.

Fisher's men were gone, Grade's professional reputation was intact, and if Fisher was pissed off that Buchanan had gotten away... the fact he had Elizabeth, once they picked her up from the hospital, and all the bitcoin they'd bought with his money had to be some consolation. Even TJ had been handed back over once Nesmith didn't need him anymore.

"You made the right call," Dory said. She set the coffee on the table in front of Grade and slid into the chair opposite him. Her hands were curled around a gaudy pink-and-yellow Lisa Frank unicorn mug she'd had since she was ten. The rim was chipped, and the handle had been glued back on, but Dad had bought it for her, so it was her cup. "Buchanan was an asshole, but he saved your life. I'll take a split lip over a dead brother… and maybe he'll get away somewhere, be a better person."

Grade took a drink of coffee. It was pretty gross. He didn't know what Dory did to perfectly good ground coffee to make the machine spit this stuff out.

"Do you really think Dad's alive?" he asked. "Out there, on the run like Buchanan."

She turned the coffee mug in her hands as she looked down into it. "Sometimes," she admitted quietly. "On good days."

"Sounds nice," Grade said.

She shrugged and took a drink of coffee. "It means I still worry about him," she said. "If he's OK. If he misses us. Sometimes, even when it's shit, I put up stuff on social media about how great my life is. So he doesn't worry if he looks us up."

Grade bit his tongue. He was trying to be nice, and this time he'd brought Dad up. That meant he didn't get to argue about how her version of their dad was an asshole.

"Will the Choke be OK?" he asked. "If you take a few days off?"

She shrugged. "Yeah," she said. "I can get some of my friends to cover, but I might just go in. I'd rather be doing something than just sit here and think about… stuff. You can't think and keep the beat. Did you know that?"

Grade shook his head. "I did not." He hesitated for a second and then set the coffee down. "Are you OK? I have… I've some stuff to sort out."

"I'm fine," Dory said. "Mom's here."

Grade nodded and got up. He kissed the top of her head before he left. Like Dad used to do.

He was halfway out the door when she cleared her throat.

"It *was* the right call," she said. "You wouldn't get away with it a second time."

"I might," Grade said. "I'm better at it now."

He locked the door behind him, just in case, and put his hand in his pocket to jangle Clay's stolen keys. That was as good an excuse—reason—as any for going to Clay's house. Grade would need to give the car back sooner or later after all.

It didn't mean anything.

§

Clay sprawled out half-naked on the bed. His jeans were unbuttoned and slung low over lean hips, and he'd kicked his boots off. Bruises covered his arms and torso, camouflaged by the scars and ink. He had half a bottle of whiskey propped against his stomach, his fingers wrapped loosely around the neck. Country music hammered out of the speakers, loud enough it made the lingering tinnitus in Grade's ears turn up a few notches.

It didn't look like he wanted company, never mind to fuck anyone.

Grade hesitated in the doorway. He'd no reason to think that he was wanted here. It hadn't exactly been a real invitation, and it definitely hadn't been a real confession.

And it wasn't his problem.

Clay cocked one leg up, faded denim pulled tight over lean muscles, his foot braced against the sheets, and took another swig of whiskey.

"You can just go," he slurred without lifting his head. "I don't need sobering up."

Grade shrugged his jacket off and walked over to the bed. He crawled onto it and lay down next to Clay.

"You know what I learned today?" he said as he tangled his fingers through Clay's. "You can't think and fuck at the same time."

Clay swallowed thickly and propped himself up on one elbow. His hair still had blood in it, matted into the curls.

"Is that true?" he asked.

Grade shrugged and reached up to curl his hand around the back of Clay's neck. "I don't know," he said. "Do you want to find out?"

There was a pause, and then Clay made a raw, desperate noise in the back of his throat. He stooped down and kissed Grade roughly, all teeth and stubble and the salty bite of fresh blood that tangled on their tongues. He only pulled away long enough to drag Grade's shirt up over his head and toss it off the bed.

Then he hesitated, braced over Grade.

"I get people killed," he said.

Grade pulled him back down. "Me too."

# EPILOGUE

**BUCHANAN RESTED HIS** plaster cast on the bar as he waved down the bartender. The lean woman ignored him as she bantered for tips, but finally the pretty people cleared and she made it down to him.

"Vodka," he said, over the heavy beat of the industrial music through the speakers. "Straight. And I was told to ask for Dmitri."

She poured them both a shot and tossed hers back without a flinch.

"That's me," she said as she wiped the back of her mouth on her hand. Blue ink curved between her knuckles and over her thumb.

Buchanan picked up his glass. The vodka smelled like something you'd use to clean paint off a brush.

"Grade sent me," he said. "Grade Pulaski."

Dmitri raised her eyebrows. "That's you?" she said. "He told me you'd be coming by."

She took the vodka out of his hand and tossed it back. Then she crooked her finger for him to follow her.

It turned out that Tommy Pulaski's little boy was a lot more connected than Buchanan had thought when they first crossed paths. Apparently he was very good at his job and had met some very interesting people.

## DIRTY WORK

The back of The Rule had women in bras pouring cheap-shit whiskey into expensive bottles. There were guns on the wall and half-finished passports laid out on a desk. From what Buchanan had picked up, Dmitri was a fixer. If you needed somewhere to go and some way to get there, Dmitri made it happen.

And Dmitri, he guessed, owed Pulaski.

"I need out of the country," Buchanan said. He pulled a wad of cash out of his pocket—what he'd been able to grab from the bag before he ran—and set it down on the desk. "Colombia eventually, but wherever I can go to start with."

Dmitri picked up the cash and nodded. "I can get you anywhere you need to go," she said. "Do it."

The garrote looped over Buchanan's head and dug into his throat. He gagged and clawed at his own skin and then behind him, at the hands that twisted the thin rope. The woman had gloves on, and his nails just raked over the leather.

"Grade said he had a message for you," Dmitri said impassively. "You shouldn't have hurt his sister."

Buchanan tried to speak up and defend himself, or maybe it was to try and bargain his way out. He couldn't tell, because the words caught below the garotte like a burp. He reached for the money as the red crawled in at the side of his vision, but the world went black before his fingers touched it.

## ABOUT TA MOORE

**TA MOORE** is a Northern Irish writer of romantic suspense, urban fantasy, and contemporary romance novels. A childhood in a rural, seaside town fostered in her a suspicious nature, a love of mystery, and a streak of black humor a mile wide.

Coffee, Doc Marten boots, and good friends are the essential things in life. Spiders, mayo, and heels are to be avoided.

TA Moore can be found at the following locations:
Blog: www.tamoorewrites.com

If you've enjoyed this book, please consider leaving a review for TA Moore on Amazon and other book retailer sites. Actually, it would be great to leave them for any book you've enjoyed. Authors truly appreciate it.

To catch up on all Rogue Firebird Press authors, please visit www.roguefirebird.com
For other TA Moore's Dreamspinner releases, visit www.dreamspinnerpress.com

*Cash in Hand*

"Cash in Hand is a fast-paced, twisty turn of a story that really kept me in its clutches to the very end."

—Love Bytes

*Hex Work (Babylon Boy #1)*

"If you enjoy a good mystery with lots of twists and turns and some surprising chemistry with some magic thrown in, I think you'll like this kickoff to Babylon Boy."

—Love Bytes

*Wanted – Bad Boyfriend (Island Classifieds #1)*

"This is the perfect comfort food… I love Moore's books and her way of writing. This author always manages to infuse warmth and humanity to both the characters and the story, as well as humor."

—Joyfully Jay

# AUTHOR CATALOG

**Published by Rogue Firebird Press
and Other Publications**

## NIGHT SHIFT

Shift Work

Split Shift

Shiftless

## ORANGE NORTHERN WOMAN SHORT STORY PRIZE WINNER

Island Life

*(Ulster Tatler)*

## ORANGE NORTHERN WOMAN SHORT STORY PRIZE FINALIST

Words of Wisdom

*(Barefoot Nuns of Barcelona
& other short stories)*

## ADDITIONAL PUBLICATIONS

Labyrinth of Stone

Red Milk

*(Requiem for the Departed)*

The White Heifer of Fearchair

*(The Phantom Queen Awakes)*

A Different Kind of Monster

*(Blood Fruit)*

## Published by Dreamspinner Press and DSP Publications

### DIGGING UP BONES
Bone To Pick

Skin And Bone

### WOLF WINTER
Dog Days

Stone The Crows

Wolf At The Door

### LOST AND FOUND
Prodigal

### BLOOD AND BONE
Dead Man Stalking

### THE PRODIGIUM
Cash In Hand

### STAND-ALONE NOVELS
Liar, Liar

Every Other Weekend

Swipe

Take The Edge Off

### ANTHOLOGIES & SHORT STORIES

Collared

*(Devil Take Me)*

Elf Shot

*(Bad, Dad, & Dangerous)*

## HEX WORK
## BY TA MOORE

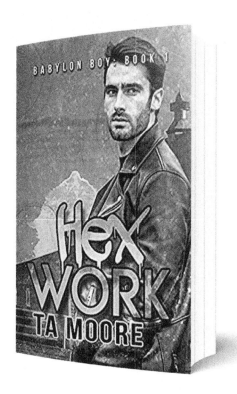

My name is Jonah Carrow, and it's been 300 days since I laid a hex.

OK, Jonah Carrow isn't actually an alcoholic. But there's no support group of lapsed hex-slingers in Jerusalem, so he's got to make do. He goes for the bad coffee and the reminder that he just has to take normal one day at a time.

Unfortunately, his past isn't willing to go down without a fight. A chance encounter with a desperate Deborah Slater, and a warning that 'they're watching', pulls Jonah back into the world he'd tried to leave behind. Now he has to navigate ghosts, curses, and the hottest bad idea warlock he's ever met...all without a single hex to his name.

But nobody ever said normal was easy. Not to Jonah anyhow.

## SHIFT WORK
## BY TA MOORE

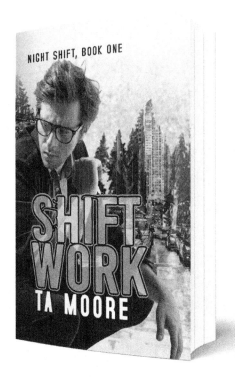

You'd think the werewolves would be the worst thing about the Night Shift; you'd be wrong.

All Officer Kit Marlow wanted was a cup of coffee and some downtime before his next night shift. Instead, he got a naked man in the elevator and an unaccounted-for dead girl in the morgue. He's going to need to deal with both before he can head for his bed.

Or anyone else's. Although not much chance of that.

Reluctantly partnered with the acerbic security consultant Cade Deacon—last seen naked in the elevator—Marlow delves into the dead girl's life. Between them, they uncover a new crime scene with the whiff of old corruption. A corruption that, five years ago, nearly took Marlow's life and ended his career.

Finding out who killed the dead girl on the slab might only be the start of this investigation. Oh, and it's the second night of the full moon. So 80% of the city, including Cade, will turn into werewolves in the middle of the case.

So, there's that.

Printed in Great Britain
by Amazon

82888806R10119